The Shade

JALAYAH JADE

ISBN: 0996070443
ISBN 13: 9780996070447
Library of Congress Control Number: 2014915548
Myrtle Beach, South Carolina

Acknowledgments

First and foremost I want to thank God. He gave me challenges and tests but with the right people by my side I have survived the storm and learned. I like to think that I turned my negatives into Blessings and utilized the talent that He gave me. Without Him nothing is possible. I also wanted to thank my personal cheer squad, my Day-One people, my Mama and Dad. I love ya'll so much that words can't even begin to describe our bond, thank you for not only always being there for me but for also believing in me...even on the days that I didn't. You both will always have me and my crazy-ass laugh by your side so let's go get it with book two and keep it movin'! Thank you for being such great role models and showing me what "grit" and hard work can accomplish, I thank Him everyday that both of ya'll are in my life! Sandra Feen, you already know that I count you as family and one of my closest friends, thank you for editing <u>The Shade</u>. If you only knew how much love and respect I have for you Sandy, I'm forever grateful for your presence. Much love. AMB Aija Monique on the cover, you did the daymn thing girl! Thank you, I love it! R.I.P to my G, I know that you're lookin' down proud and smiling. There are plenty of days that seem empty at times without your stories and laugh, we all miss you, believe that! R.I.P to my "Butterfly" who will always have a place in my soul. Fly high baby girl and stay watchin' over us all too.

Denise, you played a huge role in my life and I wish I knew where you were at in life, I'd love to personally thank you for all that you've done. Thanks. Special shout-out to my test readers! For those who have either read the first few pages or the whole rough draft. Thank you. I love ya'll for giving me both feedback and support. To everyone who cop'd their copy, much love and I appreciate it. Thanks for all of the love and support ya'll, even on these social sites. I told cha'll it was #CominToAhHoodNearYo soon, it took me longer than I had planned but thank you for staying patient! A'aight now I'm ready to present ya'll with part one of this [TRILL]ology. Meet Chantell and Jayceon.

follow me on twitter @JalayahJade

add me on facebook.com/JalayahJadeStreetLit

Chapter One

A female's voice hissed over my speakerphone. It's not Jayceon like I hoped it would be. Instead, this hood rat bitch tells me "Who the fuck is this?"

I'm used to these hos calling so I let her realize "Uh, excuse me, who tha fuck is you? Yo' called my phone! Tuh!" I rolled my eyes because it's probably some cracked out bitch trying to act like she stole Jayceon's love away, or mad because he didn't give her a deal on the rocks. But shit, me and mines gotta make our profit and these bitches always stay hating.

"It don't matter who I am cuz yo' mayne knows who I am!" She paused, really emphasizing "mayne" with her thick hood accent. Trying to talk a good game she says "I was all over his fine ass last night, suckin' his dick and he ate me out too, bitch! Did he already tell you we fucked?"

I sucked in sharp. To this hood rat bitch I had to put up a tough front but it was hard hearing that, Jayceon has cheated before and I still wonder if he creeps sometimes, but I'ma get to that in a few. Let me finish with this bitch.

"Tuh, bitch, he ain't want cha stank, crack head, nasty, STD pussy! Yo' must know who tha fuck I am, I'm Jayceon Michael's wifey, main bitch, and you ain't! He wouldn't even letchu touch his ass let alone

1

swallow, so if yo' wanna stop playin dese phone games yo' know where *we* stay! Shit, if you really wanna do somethin' bout it den be 'bout it!"

I don't have time for this shit, hanging up the phone before she tries to throw some comeback at me. What I really need is Jayceon here, filling up another Grape White Owl and making me feel like his main bitch, his Shawtie. That's how we get our paper in these Chicago Streets from the trap houses that Jayceon runs. There's one over on East 131ˢᵗ Street in the brick apartment complex, our oldest trap house over on the South Side. The newest one that we just opened over by the East Side is a tiny house off of South Avenue H. It's the grey sided house with the tiny porch and a flimsy black rod iron railing guarding the place. It's got a patch of grass out front and two windows facing the street. We got it for the low price and turned it into our own Walgreens. Of course we have our main headquarters above Rick's Corner Store off of South Lafayette Avenue. We call it Rick's after the last owner who helped us get the place. I've been here by myself for going on three days now, not knowing if Jayceon is okay and safe from the Feds, fiends and slugs. His ass never calls or texts while he's away. So, the next best thing is Dee.

Dee is technically my first cousin from my mom's only sister Glenda, my Aunt, but she's more like a sister and mother wrapped into one. She's been by my side since we've been kids with fucked up haircuts, imagining we had toys out front on empty porch steps up to now. I'll give her a call and see what she's doing. Hopefully she's not arguing with her baby's dad. Reaching for my red BIC lighter, I inhale a newly pearled blunt that was hiding out on the table and give Dee a call.

"Aye boo, what's good mama?" I could hear music in the background, it sounded like Pretty Rickey or Plies. She tells me she's doing the usual, taking care of my godchildren and fighting with her baby's dad Jamal. They always stay fighting but get back together, just like me and Jayceon. From bullshit fights about the smallest insecurities or incident to the time or two that I've caught Jayceon with a new side chick, Dee and Jamal have their rounds similar to ours. No matter what we all go through it's like we're a tight clique because through the tears and pain or pleasure we ride together. Physical fights yeah Dee and Jamal have them but not like me and Jayceon, you'll see how we get down! Once his ass finally gets home its goin' go from screamin' to hair pullin' real quick, watch. Anyway's I couldn't wait to tell Dee who the hell called me earlier, shit, I gotta keep her updated on the hood rat radar!

Clucking the roof of my mouth Dee asks me what I'm getting into tonight. Now is my chance to put that stank bitch on our hood rat radar. "Tuh, not shit, just getting prank calls from dese nothin' ass hos, you kno how dat goes…" Dee turns down the love melody and gets serious, asking me who called and who's trying to talk shit.

"I don't know her name but she was actin' like she was all ova Jay sayin' that she gave him head and he went down on her and shit…" Before I could finish Dee squealed back "Nuh-huh! Girl, that's fuckin' crazy, you think he was creepin? Cuz I swear to God, all tha shit he's done to you…" Going a mile per second she offers "Well c'mere and talk, we can play some dominoes and laugh at all dese haters and hos!" I wanted to leave this tiny one bedroom apartment with bland off white paint and have Dee give me a much needed hug. We would laugh all night and into the next day. That's how close we are, even closer before I feel in-love with one of Chi-Town's greatest hustla's on the streets. Now, I can't leave unless I get permission and Jayceon would get more than pissed at me for calling if it wasn't about business or an emergency. To leave the crib, drug money, the work, and scales behind for something as stupid as seeing Dee to play Domino's would be a huge fuck up for me. I would probably get jumped by Jayceon, it'd be a tag team match with him, his fists and the butt of his gun. I'm surprised I wasn't checked into the hospital, last time Dee had to come over and take care of me because I couldn't move for a few days. Jayceon was too busy in the streets to look at my fucked up face. That's why I have learned to play my part and do my job, its simple when he's gone. All I do is just watch over our headquarters, sell to any of the usual fiends or regular customers who beg for Jayceon or me to answer the door anytime day or night. If the Feds bust through, well I have a certain evacuation plan. I hate to tell Dee "no" especially when I would love to get out of this cooped up crib and escape the feelings that start to flood back.

"Chantell, yo' ass still dere?!"

"Yeah, I'm here Dee…But I can't come over, Jay's not here." Pausing, I take the last hit of the ruminants of the blunt, when I realize how lonely I truly am. *Damn it Jay, when are yo' comin' home baby?* I thought to myself. Dee interrupts with her interrogation.

"What? Cha'll fightin' again? Is dat why his black ass outta tha house tonight cuz I'm tellin' yo' Chantell, if that nigga lays one mo' muthafuckin' hand on yo' I'm finna have ah problem wit his hustlin' ass. And best believe I'll handle dat!" Slowing Dee down with my laughter, I tell her we ain't on no shit like that today. I can still picture her chasing Jamal outta tha house, damn well near buck naked after they fucked because he admitted he was creeping with some side chick. Dee is fucking nuts but I love her crazy ass. It's always been unsaid but if I need her to kill, all I would have to do is give Dee the word and she'd really handle that. We've been that tight since our early childhood days and still to this day.

Informing her with my cocky diva confidence "Nah, we ain't hittin'." I shake my head and finish telling Dee where he's at "shit, he's just chillin' wit Killa Kam ova at tha East Side." I laugh again at her chasing Jamal in my head and tell her "Bitch, yo' trippin'," to try and shake the tension from Dee's roughness.

"Mmhmm, yeah, I'm trippin' Chantell when was tha last time Jay treated you like his Shawtie, his main bitch or the most important bitch on the block? Huh?"

"Wow, really Dee?" She shoots back "Seriously, and don't count tha shoppin' sprees and expensive dinners either!" I looked around at all of the pictures on our wall, two smiling caramel faces wearing matching colors. He's in a Marc Ecko polo two sizes too big for his 180 lb. frame and I'm in a sexy summer dress that hugs every curve. Did I mention it was Louie Vuitton? Yeah, Jayceon keeps me looking just as fresh as him. Our trip to Virginia Beach was spectacular. Jay made some new connects, I got to see the Ocean for the first time, and as usual we were treated like hood royalty. But back to the breezy, thunderstorm Chicago reality. "Virginia beach, we was straight den…"

"Why ain't cha'll straight now?" Dee slams the question down faster than a shot of Patron.

"Uh, Dee, I'ma have ta letchu go, I've gotta headache…call me tomorrow?" I can't stand how she interrogates me. Shit. I just want Jayceon here at home with me! Even if we're busy arguing, fighting or throwing fists, I just want him home. She murmurs some bullshit "told-chu-so" line and hangs up. I curl up even tighter into a ball on the suede sofa and let the blanket bury me deeper into my thoughts. I glare at the black frames then get sentimental. We always looked so happy and in-love but I can still feel the bruises. I've been up for almost three days straight, my eyes feel like Jayceon gave me another black eye. I wish Jayceon would have had Lil Trae, one of his main niggas in our crew handle the trap situation that night. See, I really wanted to tell Jayceon that I think I'm pregnant, but I'm not too sure because I haven't taken an EPT test yet. I've played off the morning sickness by telling Jay I drank too much last night or blamed it on my cooking. My plan was to have Jay go with me to buy one at Walmart, Target or any fucking store and hold my hand every step of the way. We both want children, but, with Jayceon's main focus on the streets and hustling in the coke, 'dro and our newest edition of Perk 30's… now just isn't the "right" time. But I'm hoping deep within my heart, right under the tattoo that reads Jayceon on my chest; I pray that we're expecting.

Chapter Two

nock. Knock. Knock. The blinds hide whoever's on the narrow wooden deck, I immediately jump up and grab my Beretta. Tip-toeing to the blinds it could've been an addict, Lil Trae, Jay or the Feds…but with the after-midnight darkness, I couldn't really make out a face. To play it safe I yell "Who is it?!"

"Reeci! I need ta get a fix! Yo' ass got some Perk's on deck?" Whew, just another fiend. Unlocking the three locks and a chain I see Reeci's crater filled face. She's here for her fix of Perk 30's.

"C'mon Reeci, it's too cold for yo' skinny ass to be out 'chere." Shivering, I let her come in as far as the glass coffee table, that's the only rule. No addict or junkie can pass that coffee table that's made of thick glass and held up by a fancy French black rod-iron base. Jayceon really enforces this rule; he almost smashed Glenn's head straight thru it last summer, and luckily we had a spare one in our bedroom for a night stand. Reeci's eyes light up when what little bit of heat I have hits her weathered face. She knew a nice high was in her future which made the heat feel even closer to heaven. Rubbing her palms together she always looks around nervous like I'm part of the fucking Feds or some shit. I went into our bedroom and beside the work and scales I grabbed three pills, for Reeci's regular fix.

"A'ight Reeci, yo' want tha regular?" I say as I walk back into the living room. She's still just a few steps away from the door handle.

"Yeah, shit, I need that! Can yo' cut me a deal tho?!" If Jay was here Reeci wouldn't even try that bullshit, but she must have noticed the 300 gone.

"Nah, Reeci, dis shit ain't no T.V. show *Deal or No Deal*, c'mon now!" Her empty brown eyes begged and so did her chapped lips.

"Chantell" she whined. "Dre ain't gimmie that much money this week…" At five foot six she made a good income for Dre, her first true love and pimp. They've been together since before his gator shoes, Dayton rims, and before her dreams of Art School at CU faded into crushed pill dust and 'dro smoke. Reeci loved to paint, at least that's what she always bragged about.

Her white face looked hideous since she started the pills about a year ago. Shit, I don't even think she brushes her brown hair that just chills in a bun atop her head looking all fucked up.

"Fine. Fuck it." Crinkled up bills appear and I inspect the dough.

"Here, Reeci, stay safe a'ight!" I try to smile as she leaves.

Hell, I've got my own problems I don't need Reeci's too. After I walk her out, I quickly re-lock the door and sigh. Another re-run of VH1's *Behind The Music* starts and I keep flipping channels. It's going on five a.m. and he still ain't home. Fuck it. I'll just stay up until he gets here and he better hope he don't smell like no hoochie either because I'll catch a case this morning! I know Dee would have my bail money ready for me too.

Knock. Knock. Knock. This better not be Reeci trying want a refund or bitch about water color pastel's…before I can reach the blinds, a key rattles, and my face lights up. Swaying in smelling like Hennessey and 'dro Jayceon has his black duffel bag swung across his shoulder. The wind whips behind him, hitting my face as he steps inside. Slamming the paint chipped door he slurs "Daddy's home Shawtie!"

His duffel bag hits the floor and he scoops me up into an embrace. Our tongues collide, my tongue ring swirls around his iced out grill and instead of enjoying Jay's kiss, the way his hand smacks my round ass, the phone call from earlier pops into my head. I want to instantly hit flip mode, call him out about that trifling bitch but I realize that there's consequences to that. After hearing that hos words "who tha fuck is this" ring in my head it makes me back away. *Oh hell nah.*

"Bae what's wrong? You want me to jus bend yo' ova tha couch?!" I could feel his hard dick grind against my stomach. It felt so good to have Jay home I almost decided to not even say a word, my pussy was already so sprung from just a kiss, and I knew I could use the sex to get some of my frustration out. Jay tries to keep the foreplay going, kissing on my neck with those craving butterfly kisses. Damn. Ah nigga had me gone, almost. I pull away and head over to my lonely spot on the couch and grab my blackberry. Its ruby studded case has survived all these fights and arguments in the last year. Here's round number 421 and I hope it withstands this one, cuz Jay's going get more than pissed when I confront his ass.

"Chantell, what tha fuck?" I can tell his high is fadin' when I scream "whose fuckin' number is dis nigga?" A long ten inches in his hand, its swole and ready for me, my mouth and my wet pussy, but instead his face contorts up and he stuffs it back in his pants. Coming closer he finishes the zipper when he says with an unheard amount of innocence that Jay usually never possesses. "Who?" I put the phone all up in his grill, so close, that he probably can't even read it. He acts like it's a long-lost connect number when he still plays that innocence role. "Chantell, I don't know who dat is…?"

I scream at him like he's that ho who called earlier when I say "I don't know either, but some hood rat bitch was tellin' me she been all over you, suckin' yo' dick and yo' ate her out!" My voice starts to crumble, I want to cry and just punch Jayceon in his chest, but I need to hold it together and keep up my tough front. I mug him up and down when he starts his defense. "Yo' dumb ass goin' believe dese hos? Chantell, Bae, yo' already know I only fucks witchu…" A sly grin creeps on his face, rubbing his hands together I can tell all he wants is to get in-between my butter pecan thighs and defuse this argument. He moves closer and licks his lips, trying to lay me down on the couch and start it off when I let him know. "Nah, nigga, get off me! Yo' obviously been fuckin' wit dese tricks…Yo' let her suck your dick Jayceon?!"

Our eyes connect and lock. He's getting even more pissed that I'm not letting go of this argument, because according to Jayceon, he's to be greeted like a king when he walks in. I should've never questioned his absence, accused him of cheating, and I should understand that he's out in these streets for the paper and staying on the grind for *us*. I know that I shouldn't complain but when he leaves for three days on a simple task of checkin' on the money at a local trap, it shouldn't take no got damn three days, you feel me? Anyways Jayceon starts his shit when he roars back, already close enough to slap me in my face.

"No, Chantell, I fuckin' toldchu I don't fuck wit dese chicken head bitches!" He continues to tell me "What tha fuck is yo' mad for? Cuz I'm gone fo' three days and yo' stuck at da crib? Huh? Cuz shit I'm out cha on tha grind to elevate us, get us outta dis damn apartment and into ah mansion and all I ask is yo' hold me down thru it all. Yo' already been here dis long, you know how I am and who I am Chantell…" He starts to walk into the kitchen shaking his head when he adds "Yo' dumb ass need ta quit havin' them late night conversations wit Dee. She always puttin' that bullshit in yo' head-" Walking back over to the love seat he flops down, weary from the last few days on the grind. I'm still standing up just mumbling how this is some bullshit to myself, well actually loud enough for Jay to hear me when he sparks up and gets chest to chest with me. Looking down he scares me when he says "Yo' swear ta God what Chantell?" I swallow hard, his eyes turn ruthless and my stomach turns. This shit is going to escalade and I'm trying to back track and find a way out of this. I try to back up and move away from Jay's built six foot two frame but it's too late. Grabbing a fist full of hair, here we go again.

"Nothin'…nothin'…baby…" I mumble.

He pushes me against the dining room wall when he starts yelling.

"All I do is hustle so yo' ass can lay back." His dominate right hand snatches my face, I can't even move my jaw let alone my mouth when his tirade continues.

"Shoppin' sprees, free weed, Louie V and Chanel, and great sex… all yo' bitch ass wanna do is trip!" Shakin' his deep sea waves at me in disbelief he asks me "Where did I tell yo' ass I was goin' when I left?"

10

His grip doesn't loosen so I try to answer "East Side trap" but it doesn't come out too clear. Smack. Slap. Jayceon's whole hand flies hard and I cry out. I crumble to the ground when my tears start to pile up, I try to hide them but they slide out, my backs against the wall and Jay is staring down. Commanding me to get up he orders "Bitch, get up!" I didn't move quickly enough for his approval because he pulls me back up by my long, tangled cornrows.

"Daddy, look, I'm just tired of---" He stares deep into my eyes when his hand captures and chokes my throat.

"Chantell, I'm tired. All I do is hustle, stay on my grind, make sure tha money's straight and stay away from the Feds…All yo' can do for yo' mayne is accuse me of shit, listen to dese streets, and fuck up my high…I'm finna tell yo' ass---"

Another set of knocks stops our lecture. Squeezin' my neck tighter he jerks his hand away and heads for the door. Holding his heat tucked inside his jeans he tells me not to move unless I want round two, then unlocks the door. I try to straighten out my hair. Fuck my long braids are tangled and twisted.

"Aye what's good my nigga Lil Trae?!" Lil Trae comes in and makes himself at home on the suede sofa. Snapping his finger Jay points to our room. I hear Jay tell Lil Trae to give us ah minute as he puts his grip on the back of my neck, leading me to our room. Whipping my petite five foot frame around to face him, he finishes his lecture with a real threat. Something between a promise and a guarantee, something I truly don't want. "Keep accusin' me of shit, yo' lil ass might come up missin' or might need to find a new nigga…" He's waiting for me to say somethin' smart and I take the opportunity to think 'bout it.

I take a chance when I say all sassy "Yo' must be fuckin' wit dem hos cuz yo' always defendin' them and stay gone fo' days at ah time… nigga, I swear, I fuckin' hate yo' triffilin' ass!" He punches me in my stomach, hard as hell and I land on the bed.

Pouncing on top of me he growls "If yo' stupid ass hate me so much then leave! Get tha fuck out, pack yo' shit cuz yo' can easily be replaced!" *Jayceon knew that he was putting up a tough front, he deeply knew that there was no replacing Chantell or their whirl-wind love. He wouldn't and won't have it any other way; this is just a phase in their relationship. She'll pout a few days and come around purring saying she's sorry about that last fight. This is how it's been since day one.* Holding her arms above her head he passionately tells her "I love you, baby, I do, but I can make it happen if yo' really wanna leave." Tears still fall from Chantell's smooth caramel face, Jayceon hates to see those baby brown eyes look so sad. His plan was never to take this argument this far, but when you fuck up some-one's high on some five a.m. bullshit, well…

Kissing my neck he tastes my tears and the pain. He gives me a sweet and slow French kiss and slowly let's go of my arms when he tells me "Now, listen up babe, get that cheatin' shit outta yo' head and let's go chill wit Trae." Inviting me to hang out with one of his main part-na's I declined the invite. Gazing into his face I move my hands and make our fingers interlock when I tell Jay I'm sorry. Getting off of me with gentle caution he smacks my ass hard, "I'ma finish dis withchu later cuz Trae's out dere." Chuckling he tells me I better not act up no mo' and to get cleaned up. I quickly get off the mahogany bedspread so I can kiss the side of his neck before he goes into the next room. Whispering to his back while he walks out, I let him know that I love him and always will. I'm heading for the shower. As soon as Jay heads into the living room I can smell the weed smoke and their brotherly laughter fills the whole apartment. It makes me smile against the pain.

Chapter Three

The florescent light in the bathroom is too bright, showing reality when I don't feel like seeing it. Lifting my shirt up, I can see a bruise on my lower back from hitting the wall. His slap is still present; I can feel the heat still stinging. I strip down to my birthday suit and inspect the damage of Jayceon's destructive ass. My stomach hurts like ah muthafucker, a pain that stays and continues to be intense. Squeezing my stomach like I just got shot, I can hardly breathe. I inhale sharply and exhale. The first thing that comes to my mind is what if I am pregnant? This pain is too much to bear, maybe the hot water shining down will help ease it. Stepping into the shower two cockroach's race to the conditioner. The second one wins. Damn, I hate bugs. I told Jay to go buy some spray and shit so I can deal with it. Oh well, there's always tomorrow to deal with these nasty ass bugs. I think when the abandoned house across the street became evacuated of that nasty ass white trash that was posted up in there, their bugs came over to join the party. My purple pouf got lathered with Dove body wash. I wish Jay was in here to kiss the pain away, wash these bruises down the drain, and put my ass to sleep. Hopefully Lil Trae don't stay all night. As the water cascades down I try to envision what I would look like with a baby bump. I arch my back and push my petite stomach out, as far as I can go and hold it. Growing up I had to live with my mom's sister and her kids, along with Dee, ever since I was around nine or going on ten. So having a child of my own, someone to love and take care of, would be a blessing for me and Jayceon. I'm hoping it would get him to slow down moving weight, keep his grind to a decent pace and not in overdrive. The hot water stings my face from when he put his hands on me. I wish he wouldn't have put his hands on me like that, but that's a small price to pay to be his wifey. I love him too much to pack my bags and leave like he offered earlier, I love his ghetto ass too much. I'd do a bid for him, rob a bank, anything, to keep Jayceon Michaels my one and only main nigga. Stepping out of the shower dripping wet, I grab my towel and dry off. I get laced up in my red velvet colored Vicky C's v-string and I leave the matching bra off. Putting on one of Jay's oversized white tees I tuck myself into bed. Their laughter and x-box playin' asses carry on in the living room. I try to sleep, but my face still feels fucked up from earlier, so I opened the nightstand drawer and grab a Vicodin. This should knock me out, help all of my pain go away, and start tomorrow off right. The last thing I remember singing in my head before falling asleep was the Tupac classic hit "Me and My Girlfriend."

Chapter Four

Stretching across the mahogany sheets my shaved kitty kat purrs for Jayceon as I wrap my leg around his. It feels wonderful to be in the same bed with my man. I was surprised he didn't jump my ass last night after Lil Trae left. Did he leave? Rubbing my hand up and down his chiseled, naked, chest he's acting like he's sleepin'. I've gotta fix that for him and I got just the solution! Gently lifting the covers I glance down and he's only wearin' boxers, it's time to wake my man up the proper way. Grabbing his morning wood I start stroking all ten inches and get him excited before I go down. Moaning in his sleep now I know this nigga is faking so I get by his right side and start off with lickin' and French kissing. Jay loves that shit. Licking from the base all the way up I finish it with putting his hefty head in my mouth. Slurrpin' and suckin' like it's a tootsie roll pop I can feel Jayceon start to prop himself up. He enjoys watchin' my A-Game head game. Grabbing a fist full of my braids I've got his full attention when he tells me "Oooh, shit. Damn mama look at chu Shawtie." He adds "Don't start nothin' yo' ain't tryin' finish" while he pushes me down more and more. Taking my tongue and licking back and forth across his oversized dick while I bob up and down I can tell Jay's ready to cum. His moans and growls get intense while my mouth inhales his too proud manhood. "Ahh, suck it like dat Ma!" Getting up I re-position myself on my knees and give slow butterfly kisses to his peach size balls. Lickin' them up like he does my pussy I make eye contact with him. He starts to give himself a hand job I let his dick slap my tongue and he tells me "Oh, shit, Bae, damn I'm cumin' why don't yo' swallow dis" Taking a good six inches to the mouth his warm juices bust into the end of my throat; it's the breakfast of champions. Raising up I whisper to him if Trae is here. He shakes his head no and gives me that look that's kept me for all these years. A look that excites me, it's the look he gives in only a few situations and make-up sex is one of 'em.

"So, is dat it Babe, all you goin' do is let me getta taste…?" I rub his chest and give him a challenge.

I kept challenging him, with me talkin' all this shit he'll have to take control. "Cuz, with all dat fighting and shit, I think I need dat ass disciplined…but, I don't know if you can handle all dis ass nigga" Giving him a teasing kiss he snatches my face the same way he did against the wall yesterday.

He growls back in his street appointed voice "Oh yeah, dat's whatchu think…I keep dis ass in check, and we both know dis!" Smiling he gives me a heart stopping kiss, every time we kiss like that I swear to God it's like the fiends are in the backyard lettin' fireworks off. It's fucking magical. Jayceon lifts me up, my legs wrap around his waist and he gently pushes me against the bedroom wall. Holding onto my oversized ass his arms keep me scooped up while we kiss. Moving to my breasts he gets a taste and nips at my overly excited flesh.

"Mmhmm Daddy, look at chu handling dis ass!" I squeal with excitement because it's been too long, we both need this!

"Shit, I just started Bae, you ready fo' me to eat dat pussy out?" He asks me in-between a long French kiss while I moan.

"Mmhmm…yeah, baby, c'mon!" I scream with such a craving delight. Carrying me over to the bed and he lays me down on my back, oh shit, we 'bout to get it in. Going for my thighs he works his way down, taking his time with the kisses and taking mouthfuls on my natural D cups. He calls them my fruit cups because once he starts sucking on my nipples and circling around them with his tongue it means my love is about to cum down. Jayceon has me panting, but that's not good enough for my hustla, he likes to make me beg for it. With my thighs wide open and he's on the floor he instructs me "Play wit dat pussy for me baby."

Sticking my index finger in my mouth I suck on it just like I did his dick and start to do the manual work, I hope this shit don't last long because I've been doin' this too much lately. He needs to just break me off and stop fuckin' round with this foreplay. I play his game though and purr back "Just like dat Daddy?" His eyes scan my face and nod then he's hypnotized by my wetness. Giving a light moan while I toss my head back and let my body really relax he loses control. Pushing my hand back he slides two fingers in and I arch back, I let his fingers take me for a spin around tha block, rocking with his motion and I can hear his breathing pick up. It's crazy how when he touches me I get crazy wet like I need to throw a life jacket to him, when I'm by myself I never get *this* wet. My "oohs" and "aahhs" turn into my legs shaking and I get minez without him even putting the tip in. Pulling my ankles closer to him, my legs fly up quick and his mouth gets more than a taste when Jay goes down. Licking up and down on my hot box, his whole mouth devours my pussy and I'm so gone all I can do is scratch the sheets, I keep gasping until he makes me bust another nut. Making me taste his drenched tongue, he gets on top and asks me "Yo' tryin' ryde dis dick mama? Can you handle this?" We switch positions again, he gets on the bed and lays back waiting for the show to pop off. Getting up I go over to the bedroom door, Jay asks me where I'm going and I tell him I was 'bout to get some music. I needed something to ride to. I head out the room and do a quick double take to see if Lil Trae was on the couch or in the kitchen. Jayceon has told me before that no one was in the house and as soon as I go out there's Trae or Kam there or some random person on the couch, but this time I honestly didn't even care if someone was in the living room. Hell for all I care Lil Trae could be passed out on the couch, playin' x-box or fightin' with some trick on his phone cuz I was ready to get minez. Seeing Jayceon's phone, yeah that will do, I'm sure he's got some type of baby making music on here. Snatching it off the counter I return back to our room. Oh shit. What if Trae was in the bathroom? I'm glad he didn't walk out if he's here when I passed through. I slam the bedroom door and find Plies "Please Excuse My Hands" and set the phone on the dresser. I can tell Jay's getting upset because I'm taking too long, he thinks I'm avoiding this good-lovin' but I'm just tryin' make sure it's some of the best we've had in a few months. Im finna show his ass why he comes back home to wifey. The chorus starts and I twerk all the way over to Jay, his dick pops up at attention again and he's coaxing me to come closer so he can pull me over, get me on top quicker but I want to make *him* beg for once. Pop locking and dropping it, I feel like I should be at June Bugs on the pole when he gets off the bed and lets it dangle in my face. Since yo ass ain't goin' ryde den gimmie head and I'mma smash on dat ass from tha back!" I hate when Jay gets impatient. Stroking it with my hands I look up and tell him "I was getting warmed up, I just wanted to getchu excited Bae!" Smirking he lets me kiss it once or twice and pulls me up while he sets on the bed and throws me on top his lap. I push him back on the bed and he goes along with it, moving my hips back and forth he starts to make those love faces and I hit reverse cowgirl. Slapping my ass while I ride he's enjoying the show and I must admit, I love when we have that good make-up sex. Scratchin' my back he knows that shit drives me crazy and I start to ride like I'm in the derby. "Ahh, shit, mama, look at chu," sounding winded he sets back up and starts to do some of the work, cradling my fruit cups and kissing my neck. "Yo' ready fo' Daddy to smash?" I wanted to give Jayceon a show-stopping performance but his impatient ass always gotta fuck something up. I give in to his offer, I know at the end of the day he'll always come back home, he knows dis is his pussy, and I know that I'll always have Jay's heart. We both stop the friction and get up, he lets me get on all fours and I make my ass clap. It would've been sexier if I had some heels on. We both finish to bliss after another hour of slow and fast grinding.

The shower rains down on us, we're still kissing when Jay tells me his schedule for the day. "A'ight lil mama, today I've gotta meeting wit the weed man, you know, Shawn, at three. Den I needa go check on Killa Kam." Getting soaped up Jayceon took the job of washing it off of me with his hands. I take the axe and start to get Jay cleaned up when I ask him what does he want for dinner? I was hoping that this would be an invitation for a nice dinner and a chance to tell Jayceon about my baby news, just the thought of being pregnant has got me so damn excited. Instead of a dinner reservation or going to Uno's or Joe's Crab Shack he shakes his head "no."

"Sorry Bae but I've gotta handle some business tonight and plus don't we got food here?" Massaging my tense shoulders I shake my head and say "nah, not really…"

"Why yo' ass lyin'?" He laughs and says he'll give me some money to go grocery shopping. Changing the subject with a pout while he steps out I let the rest of the water pour down on me.

"Well fine den Jay, I've gotta go get numbers today anyways so while I'm out I'll grab some take out. I hate to go grocery shopping; you know that's *our* job. I never get whatcha like." Knowing that's a lie, I grin because I usually keep the house stocked with Jay's favorites especially 'round the first and fifteenth. Jay throws on a crisp pair of Sean Johns and an all black tee, so baggy that it conceals his piece. A fresh fitted hat with his favorite team Atlanta pulls the look together. I can hear Jay callin' Lil Trae on two-way while I get ready for the day. I'm dressed in my Dior jeans with a sexy baby tee, matching belt, you know the real thin belts and before I head out the door I'll throw on my puff jacket, all black to match the forces and pull the whole 'fit together. I hear Jayceon talking but it sounds like he's on the phone, now he's yelling.

"Yeah, Trae, I got sumthin' fo' dat lil nigga! I told him 'bout doin' dat shit while he was sellin' see I told Kam dat's why yo' don't fuck with these addicts and try to help 'em out. Psssh, just wait til I kiss Shawtie bye, it's 'bout to be bed time fo' dat nigga!" Racing outta the bedroom I can see Jay's blood pressure on the rise while he's shakin' his head in disgust. I was hoping he would be in a good mood since we just made love but the pressure of the streets has got him gone. I just hope he's not on no bullshit of tryin' go to war, I need him here, I'm not tryin' see my baby get shot or caught up with some snitch shit. That's what we don't like. Shoving his phone back in his deep jean pocket he goes

19

back into our room and I can hear the sounds of the clicking noise coming from the safe.

"Chantell, here ma how much ya need?" Holding a rubber band stack with all hundreds I don't answer fast enough, I can tell his mind's racing because he rips out four bills and throws the rest back in. The safe's tough door talks back while it slams and Jay puts the bills in my hand. Rushing past me he finds his shoes and tie's 'em tight. Instead of his Flights he puts on his Timbs, I can tell some shit's bout to go down.

"A'ight, Daddy, I'll cook you ah good meal tonight, what time yo' want me to get food done? Is Trae and Kam comin' over too?"

I try to ease the tension while he lets me know "I don't know what time I'm finna be back through ma. Just cook and save me some, I've gotta handle dis lil wanna-be jack boy today." Lost in his own thoughts he doesn't answer if Trae or Kam is coming over so I take it as a "no." Standing in the door frame I ask Jayceon two more questions, I feel like a little kid seeing if my best friend can spend the night.

"Jay, baby, can Dee come ova and I need to get my hair and nails done too--" Glancing back he says "yes" to the nails and hair but "no" to Dee's company.

"Ya'll stay on dat damn phone, why yo' need her beside ya? I got shit to handle Shawtie. Just take care of dinner and if I'm not home by tomorrow then yeah she can come over...go grab numbers today and call me when yo' ass done. Stay safe baby girl." Kissing me, he pulls away and is on a mission for the 300. I watch Jayceon leave until he's out of sight. The freezing cold air makes my nipples hard and I wish he was still here, snowed in with a bottle of Ciroc or Patron. Shutting the door and locking it I think to myself *damn it, why does he always have to hustle, why couldn't he just take a damn day off or somethin'?*

Chapter Five

The South Side trap is my first stop, and dayum they're packed! It looks like we havin' an auction or on *Storage War's* and who ever bids the most gets the shitty apartment and all the drugs inside. I wonder what the fuck's going on. Racing up the sidewalk I can see the "manager" of this trap, Ray-Ray, arguing with a real young teen in the front yard. She's a white girl, which isn't uncommon on the South Side, but she's got the heart to argue with crazy-ass Ray-Ray. Now that's a mistake; I hope he don't pistol whip this bitch, or worse. "Yo' killed my mama! Yo' fuckin' killed her with dat shit chu sell!" She's all up in Ray-Ray's face pointing fingers and the neighbors are on their porches or standing in the street taking bets. Who's going to throw the first fist, get escorted off the property or end up on the ground? Let's hope no one gets shot.

I try to ease into the situation and calm it down before it can escalade. Jayceon would be proud of me when I step in and say "Ray-Ray, what's good?"

Trying to divert his attention from the one hundred and ten pound chick, he says "Nah, this bitch got me fucked up Chantell."

I announce to the audiences on the porches that stand by the curb in front of us, as well as to the two of them, "Ay, let's take this inside, we don't need no attention drawn to us, c'mon lets go take a seat inside and we'll talk."

The tiny white girl throws her hands up and yells "I'm not going in that death trap apartment! You could kill me or I could get raped! I don't know what's in there!" Trying to motion her to shut up and c'mon inside she screams louder "Bitch, I'll be back and so will my niggas! We goin' ryde on ya'll. Stay strapped up!" Storming off she hops into a beat up Honda and speeds away. I go inside and see a strung out bitch on the couch, nodding off and on, beads of sweat collect on her hairline.

Slamming the front door he screams "Fuck that bitch!" I can tell Ray-Ray's pissed, but whose momma died? Why is she puttin' our business for these nosy ass neighbors to watch? What'd that lady OD on? Shaking my head I want to dive into questions but I try to give Ray-Ray time to cool off. He lights up another blunt he must've just finished pearling before the drama popped off. Inhaling the good and exhaling the crazy he starts to tell me about the OD incident. "I've gotta let Jayceon know what happened, so if these nigga's tryin' ryde we can hit 'em up!" I let Ray know that I'll inform Jay once I leave. If he will let me find out the story I'll pass it along, word for word I promised. Ray-Ray get's into his hand motions. That's the funny thing 'bout him, anytime he get's deeply involved in a conversation you see his hands waving around like he's stranded on an island; the blunt smoke is his smoke signal. "Shit, that bitch is just mad cuz her mama was addicted to them '30's and she was a drunk. I don't think that's what killed her though. See what did it was when she came over here, aching for a high and I told her one line of this coke and two of dem pill's will getcha faded. She did four lines of coke and three pills before I really noticed. See, we've been busy lately over chere'…" Ray-Ray continues to tell me that she didn't have any money to pay him for the drugs she took, so she offered him sex and he said hell nah, he don't need her pussy he gets plenty from his own bitches. So since that trick didn't work, he had to teach her a lesson like Jay and Kam does to these fuck boys out here. A backhand smack turned into a punch and she got a lick off. If I look close enough I could see where his lip got busted. Ray-Ray has a bad temper so it was done with. Ray-Ray got his anger out, and, well, she didn't wake up. Running my hands to smooth my braids out I let the 'dro smoke sway out. I need to get these numbers quick and call Jayceon. I tell Ray-Ray it'll be a'ight and he gives me inventory and reassures me he didn't mean to kill that bitch. I would believe him if it wasn't for his temper.

I get back in the whip and make sure the Beretta's under my seat. Just in-case someone tries to fuck with me, this shit just got real and I'm finna survive these streets. I call Lil Trae and ask for his advice while I drive to the next trap. I hope that Jayceon's hanging out over there so I can inform him.

"Ay what's good my nigga?" I can hear the weariness in Trae's voice. He's probably faded off a few pills and one too many blunts.

"Not shit sis, what's up withcha? Where yo' at?" Trae slurs.

"I'm on my way to the East Side, takin' inventory and shit. Where you at cuz I need to talk to you! Some shit just popped off over on the South Side and yo ain't goin' believe what happ-" Before I could finish he fills in my words. He knew about the incident with Ray-Ray and tells me he just got off the two-way with him. "Oh, shit. Well, what should we do? Do we need to stay strapped up? Do you think he killed that bitch on purpose? Why would she do that much coke if she's never tried it? Has she tried that shit before?"

Lil Trae tells me that "Chantell, you know we all stay strapped!" I did feel safe with the pistol right beside me, in case I did need to pull the trigger. I smiled while Trae finished saying "Yeah, we don't need to worry that lil girl that was arguing wit Ray-Ray, she knew her mama was an addict. She was just tryin' to make a scene to look hard, get some frustration out, and to see if he'd pay her to go away...Yo' know dese hos be steady thirsty for some paper."

"Amen to dat Trae!" I pulled up to the lil house sitting towards the end of the street and I smile, Trae closes the phone and waves at me from the porch. *Damn, I'm glad Killa Kam ain't chere*, I scream inside my head.

Stepping inside, the frigid air wraps around me and so do my cramps. They've been somewhat calm today or maybe I didn't notice them with all the drama that's been popping off today. Anyways, I can feel 'em now and Lil Trae has to help me inside. By the time I make it to the black worn-out leather couch the pain really kicks in. Holding my lower stomach, Lil Trae asks me what's wrong. "Ahh, shit, damn, I don't know…but it's been hurting!"

I'm doubled over on the couch, wincing when he asks "Is it somethin' yo' ate? Or is it yo' time of tha month?" All I can do is shake my head "no" and Lil Trae disappears into one of the other rooms. He returns with his plastic cup filled with what looks like Hawaiian Punch but I know there's liquor in there, a pill in hand, and he comes back in to grab my pen and pad. "Here Shawtie, I'ma go take this inventory for yo' and we're goin' get up outta cha'…" I look at him puzzled, what do you mean we're leaving? Where are we going? That's what I want to ask but before I can I hear him counting out-loud, Jeezy is in the background rapping from his phone and this pain's so deep I can't even focus. I can't try to protest, Lil Trae grabs my Coach bag, the one he bought me from 2011 the Poppy Spring Collection and helps me up. We're off in his whip when he informs me "I'm takin' yo' to the ER, Shawtie you've got blood right there." He points to the spot in-between my thighs, I'm surprised I didn't faint. Oh my God.

Lil Trae weaves through the traffic, speeding in and out of cars and pulls up to the front door quicker than a delivery driver. Hopping out he tells me "Stay here right quick, I'ma grab a wheel chair fo' yo'" and leaves the car running. A nurse comes out. The wind almost steals her away and the wheel chair acts like her anchor that's helping her weather the wind, as well as rescue me from this sea of confusion. Struggling to get out of the Deville, a fat ass nurse with "exit-sign" red hair yanks on my arm and pulls me down to the chair. I should've left my all tan Coach Bag, the one with the bright pink magenta flowers in Lil Trae's car or with him, but I'm in a whirlwind of shock. Why am I bleeding? What is causing these cramps? Does Jayceon know that I'm here? Has Lil Trae told him yet? And what time is it? I can't interrupt his meeting. I'm flipping the fuck out, so my purse automatically goes with me. I hope Lil Trae's not too high to remember to keep the heat in his whip. Before I can say 'bye to Trae she's rushing me inside and Lil Trae acts like a valet.

The nurse drives me into the heart of the hospital. I by-pass all of the other sick or wounded patients and I'm at an examination room. A curtain is drawn around me and the nurse starts asking me questions. "When did the pain start? Are you pregnant? Have you been tested for a pregnancy? Are you currently taking any medication ma'am?" A little over five thousand dollars, twenty eight grams of some good Cali 'dro and a whole lotta pills accompany me to my visit in the ER where I found out the bad news...I had a miscarriage.

As I continued to sob, I can't believe I had the chance to become a mother and I lost it that quick. Meanwhile, this stupid ass nurse keeps asking me questions. All I want right now is Lil Trae to take me home, have Jayceon comfort me all night and smoke the fattest blunt that we can roll. I just want the chance to be a mommy to come back to me. Give me the chance to grow my belly bump and nurture my seed...

"Chantell, Ms. Saunders, are you okay?" She asks in a monotone voice. My whole body is shaking. Tears are flooding me away from reality. Shit, I'm still in shock. I try to calm down enough to answer "yes" but all I can do is shake my head and gulp for air. Am I having a panic attack?! "I have some questions that I would like to ask you, before you leave, is that okay?" She gives me a few minutes to calm down and then starts off by asking me how long I've been with Jayceon and how old we were when we got together.

"We've been together fo' five years and some change. When we met back in the day I was fifteen and at a party that he was throwin' fo' one of his main dudes... it was a lil party for coming home from doing a bid, I had seen him 'round my Aunt's neighborhood a few times before that. Jayceon turned seventeen that summer. Why?"

"Have you ever had a miscarriage before?" I shake my head no.

"I've never been pregnant before. Jayceon is my one and only..."

"This might be too personal and however you answer my next question will be kept between us..." I swallow hard. Does she know of all the street value that's inside my Coach Poppy purse? Did she go through my shit when I was too busy crying my eyes out with my head in-between my hands, feeling like I was enduring a panic attack? I pictured me and Jayceon inside our bathroom staring at the EPT test resting on the sink. Why couldn't these tears be happy ones, tears from an EPT test saying I'm baby momma status?! Why does Jayceon have to take shit so far with these arguments, I mean damn, he needs to stop putting his muthafuckin' hands on me! I zone back in as she continues to say "Are you in an abusive relationship? Because if you are, Chantell, we can get you away from that situation safely..." I can't believe this bitch has enough nerve to ask me this! Is she serious? I am considered hood royalty, hated by all these hos and hood rats who try and take my place, as well as respected to these hustla's as Jayceon's wifey. Does she realize who Jayceon Michaels is in these Chicago streets?!

I answer back with a solid and strong "No, I am not in that type of relationship! What would make you even ask that, what's that have to do with *us* losing *our* baby?"

Her eyes wonder to the bruises from last night's fight, the dark circles under my eyes and all of the designer shit that I'm rockin'. She glances at my nice ass brand new purse and then quickly adds "Chantell, I want to let you in on a little secret..." I just mug her up and down like she's lost her mind. "Between me, you and those pastel flowers on your Coach purse...I was in an abusive relationship with my ex-boyfriend. He used to take arguments and turn them into brawl matches, his temper was as bad as an Irishman's and so was his alcohol problem. I blamed myself for years, *always* finding a reason why it was my fault and what *I* did wrong." The attractive blonde haired nurse looks off into the distance, probably still remembering the sting of a backhand when she quietly puts all of her attention on me. "I used to be addicted to the drama, I thought that I loved him, but Chantell, love doesn't and shouldn't physically hurt. Love is not a slap, another argument over who gets the last cigarette or who is allowed to control the other person's life. Love doesn't have to be that way. It's been two years since I've changed my life around for the better!" A huge smile of perfectly straight white teeth gleam back at me. She tells me how she went to school, got her degree for some medical bullshit and now look where she's at. It's an inspiring story I have to admit, but that school shit ain't for me. I don't need no degree, I got my schooling from the streets and make my salary from these trap houses.

"Well, I'm glad that you're happy but I'm fine. Jayceon and I are great...I'm ready to go."

Standing up from her stool on wheels she takes a heavy breathe and lets me know in a motherly tone "Chantell, this is a cycle. If you don't stop this cycle no one will. Your significant other will continue this abusive cycle and as the years pass it will become more chaotic, more depressing days than the "good ones" and soon, if you stay long enough, you won't even remember who you are." She stares deep into my eyes as if she's trying to save my soul from the devil himself. The last thing she tells me before I leave is "If you're ever tired of the cycle, call me. Here's my card." She extends her latex glove towards me and a business card has her perfect smile and perfect life on it.

I decline her card telling her "I ain't in no damn cycle, me and Jayceon are fine and if yo' don't mind I would like to grieve about my loss!" Snatching my purse off the exam table like a hos weave, I made a beeline for the door and leave her behind. Searching through the hallway to find the nearest exit door, all I want is to try and find Lil Trae. He's posted out in the waiting room looking irritated, I hope he left his heat in the car, cuz we don't need no problems in here.

"Yo' good Shawtie?" He looks at me from head to toe twice.

"No. let's go," I whisper.

Wrapping his brother-like arms around me we walk to his '03 Cadillac Deville sittin' on Dayton rims. The sky looks stormy, like it's about to pour-down, just like I do when I get inside Trae's whip. It's like I've heard the news for the first time all over again when I try to tell Lil Trae. He holds me tight and soothes me from the driver's seat. It seemed like hours passed while I cried and Lil Trae kept repeating "Ssssh, its okay lil mama you goin' be a'ight. Everything will be okay, we can work through it."

Chapter Six

Lil Trae pulls into the busy Speedway gas station and finds a parking spot away from all of the crazy drivers and a safe space for his Caddy. If someone would hit one of his car doors or pull into a space too fast it'd quickly be a crime scene and on your local news tonight at eleven. Opening the passenger's side door he pulls some money out of his pocket. Knowing that Jay doesn't usually give me money while I'm just doing the task of inventory he asks me what I want from the gas station and tells me he'll pay for it.

"Nah Trae it's cool. I'm finna go in here and grab some Mountain Dew, a few packs of Marlboro's and some shells, cuz after this bullshit I'm defiantly blazing!" Still wiping my eyes Trae insists.

"Chantell, I gotcha lil mama! Let me splurge and hook yo' up, yo' know yo' my lil sista!" He jokingly pulls on my braids, tugging at them to make me smile and it works. I give him a cheesy eight year old smile then get out and head inside. I still got my hair and nail money from earlier this morning. Oh, fuck! I forgot I've got to hit the grocery store still and cook dinner. Damn it! I hurry up and grab a twelve pack and make my way straight for the cashier when my phone starts singing Mary J. Blige's "Be Without You."

"Hello?" I try and talk while throwin' the hefty twelve pack on the red scratched-up plastic counter.

"What's good Bae? Where you at?" I can tell from the music that Jayceon is over at the South Side trap. All Ray-Ray listens to is Eminem or other white-boy rappers like Haystak and Jelly.

"I'm wit Trae. Why the fuck are yo' worried 'bout it?" I wanted to tell him more but I'm still upset and pissed at him. I know he can hear it from the tone of my voice and how short of an answer I gave him.

"Oh, fo'real yo' goin act like dat!" He barks back.

I roll my eyes and tell the lady behind the counter to "Throw in dem Grape White Owls too, I need three packs!"

I hear the impatience in his next question when he asks me "When yo' comin' home boo? I got a lil surprise fo' you mama..." I breathe hard and still act like an ungrateful bitch.

"Okay, and? I'm finna be home in ah lil' bit..." That'll piss him off because usually Jayceon knows where I'm at, what I'm doing and when I'm doing it. Not today.

"See there yo' ass go with dem smart-ass answers, that's what the hell I'm talkin' bout!"

"Jayceon, I'm in line so unless yo' got somethin' to really say..."

Before I could hear his response and probably change his mind about whatever surprise he's got for me the bitch behind me screams "Can yo' ass hurry up, bitch I got places tuh go!" I swerve my whole body around and mean mug her, my phone stays glued between my ear and my left hand. This bitch might get her head slammed into this counter if she keeps talkin' that shit.

"Bitch, who the fuck is yo'? Huh? Shut the fuck up, I'm payin' and yo' dumb ass don't need to worry 'bout what I'm doin' up here any muthafuckin' ways. Tuh!" I whip my hair around and a few braids swung across her personal space. She's still behind me cussin' under her breath when I whip back around. "If you really got somethin' to say then say it to my face ho! What's good bitch?! If yo' tryin' throw hands there's a parkin' lot a few steps away, shit, lemmie finish payin' and get off the phone with my hustlin' husband Jayceon Michaels..." I'm muggin' her and I'm sure the other five people behind her don't appreciate the argument. They just want to buy their cigarettes, beer, or put ten on pump seven. She starts to say some dumb ass comeback when the clerk takes us both back to reality.

"Ma'am. Ma'am. Ay, sweetie it's $45.89"

I pull out the nail and hair money that Jayceon gave me this morning and whip it out. Laying my phone on the counter to grab the change and put it back into my purse, I yell facing towards the annoyed cashier "Yeah, my nigga keeps stacks on deck so I ain't trippin' bout spendin' fifty at the store, unlike these nasty ass tricks behind me!" I finished putting my money back into my purse and put the goods in there too. Gripping the twelve pack I ask Jayceon if he's still there. As he starts to ramble on I tell that hood rat behind me as we brush shoulders "Yup my nigga keep stacks on deck, bitches get cha' paper up!" Laughing past the others in line I make my way to the automatic sliding glass doors and Jayceon applauds me.

"Look at chu lil mama showin' these hos whose in charge!" He continues to say "So, where you and Trae at? Cuz I was finna tell you that I've gotta surprise." I carry on with our conversation like nothing in there ever happened.

"Oh yeah, well, I'm at Speedway wit Lil Trae…Did yo' hear 'bout Ray-Ray's situation today?" I start to lighten up because I hate being mean to Jayceon, especially if his ass got a surprise or something special in store for me. My baby tells me that he already knows, Lil Trae called him earlier. Did Lil Trae tell him I was in the ER today? Oh my God what if Jayceon flips? How did his meeting go with Shawn today? All these questions race into my head and make me forget about the ugly bitch behind me in the gas station.

Making my way over to Trae's whip he informs me "Chantell, Babe, I'm sorry 'bout last night. I ain't really mean to get all crazy and shit, ya feel me? I need ta control myself mo' and I was in tha wrong fo' dat stupid shit…when yo' come home I wanna make it up to yo' mama…" I was totally shocked, Jayceon hardly admits he's wrong let alone be the first one to say sorry. Damn, did Lil Trae tell him what happened and he's sugar coating my feelings? Will he hold me all night and tell me errything will be a'ight as we curl up? I hope this surprise is a good one. Hopefully he'll take me somewhere nice and I can let him know what happened.

"Wow, yo' ass neva say sorry! Tuh, why yo' bein' all apologetic and shit?" I play my role of being a harsh down-ass bitch, and it's tricky, but it keeps Jayceon on his feet.

"Fo 'real dat's how yo' feel Shawtie? C'mon now let Daddy make it up in erry lil way…I'll start by kissin' on dem fruit cups and work my way down to dat wet pussy-"

"Jayceon Michaels! Oh, damn, boo yo' nasty!" I laugh and start to blush because I'm back in the car with Lil Trae; he shakes his head and starts to back up.

I tell Jayceon we'll be home in a few and I let him know "Do yo' think yo' deserve ah chance to make it up?"

He growls back "Shit, chu betta let me make it up…" Before we hang up he adds "And, I feel bad fo' puttin' dis stress an bullshit on ya instead of dis dick…" He laughs and we finally hang up.

As Trae backs up the Caddie I spot that ho scanning the parking lot trying to see which whip I got in. Our eyes lock and before she can even do anything I flip her off. Trae laughs and he squeals out of the busy parking lot. Her face gets all scrunched up and makes the craters on her face almost form into one pill popping eye rolling cringe as I light up a cigarette. I've already sucked down that cigarette and let the second one's smoke swirl in Lil Trae's whip and out the window, just like that nurse's questions that are runnin' through my head from earlier. Trae asks me who that chick was from the Speedway and I tell him just a pill popping ho who ain't got shit on me. We both laugh and Trae starts to take us home.

Chapter Seven

"Yo' know why Jay's takin' yo' out to hit tha malls right?" Lil Trae whips 'round the corner and coasts down the block. I shake my head no when he says "He feels bad…" I give him that look like uh-huh, why would he feel bad? Lil Trae continues to tell me when he shifts the whip into park "He feels guilty Shawtie. I ain't tryin' to make you feel sad and shit ma, but Jay feels guilty 'bout snappin' and shit from that night ya'll got into it. He was just tellin' me earlier how he knows that he shouldn't treat you like he does these other bitches. You're his main chick and his ride or die; Jayceon finally sees that you could be the one." Before I can ask him if he's already told Jay about the miscarriage he assures me "Nah, in case you were wondering I ain't tell Jay about the baby news, but I'm finna put it this way, I think that Jayceon just feel guilty 'bout how he do treat chu sometimes. He's ready to make yo' wifey sometime cuz he's quit fuckin' wit dese hos. Shawtie just be patient and put it in yo' mayne's hands. He loves you and you love him…Let God do tha rest." I just stare at Trae like he's my preacher on these streets and he gives me a quick hug. Telling me he loves me like an older brother would, he snatches his cup from the holder and takes a huge sip, then grabs my twelve pack. I guard my purse around my shoulder as he leads the way up to the apartment where we met an overly nice Jayceon. I hope that I can take advantage of Jay and get some nice new shit from the mall, a nice dinner date and some great sex, my way. I just hope Lil Trae fades onto the couch so it can be just me and my baby.

"Hey what's good?" He gives Lil Trae the usual dap and goes into the kitchen to put my twelve pack up. I just stand in the door way and slowly make my way inside. "What's good mama?" Inhaling my whole body he scoops me up and gives me a quick, sweet kiss. "What's tha numba's at *our* traps lookin like today?" I pause and Lil Trae takes his usual spot on the couch, rollin' up another blunt.

"Dey was a'ight…"

Jayceon asks me "what do *we* need to re-up on?"

I notice now how he's making this hustle into ours and not just his. This has to be a part of his Mr. Nice Guy plan. But, honestly I'm still pissed at him from last night's fight. Shit, if he didn't take it that far I could still have the chance to be a mom. If Jayceon hadn't treated me like one of his hood rat bitches I would be labeled "baby mama" status and he'd probably propose. Then we could get married and it'd be official in the streets. I would be Jayceon Michael's main bitch, wifey, and baby's mom which is all that I've ever wanted. But, not now, not since that fight, and damn if that nosey ass bitch's questions still weren't inside my mind. As I try to sort out my thoughts, trying to honestly ask myself am I in an "abusive relationship" type shit, Jayceon is steadily screaming at me.

"Chantell! Chantell! What the hell are yo' doin'? Didn't you hear me askin' yo' to get your purse?" I shake my head no and automatically grab the bag off of the floor. Grabbing his trap house profits, re-up money and some pills he goes into our bedroom and I take a seat with Lil Trae. He's on the phone with somebody. It sounds like his dude Swoop or JD; those are Trae's real blood brothers.

I space out. I guess that I'm still in shock of it all. I can't believe that I had the chance to be Jayceon's baby's mom and wifey and in the blink of an argument, one fist, and some crazy ass words, it's gone. That nurse with her perfect face is still in my head and there's no way that she can relate to me and my life. She probably hasn't even left the burbs let alone live in a trap house or see these fiends on a daily basis!

Shit, that bitch don't know me and Jayceon like Dee or Trae does. Now if they would say that same shit she did, it might be different. At least I hope it would.

I don't even notice Jayceon hovering around the couch until he answers his phone "Who tha fuck is dis?!" I don't even care who it is; I'm still intertwined in my own thoughts. Lil Trae grabs a cup of ice and pours some of the Beam left from a few weeks ago making another strong drink. I left the Beam there because I thought that I was becoming a mother. I didn't want to drink like my mom did when she was pregnant with me. It feels like hours before Jayceon finishes with the numbers from both traps and counts all the money. Did he count those pills yet? I think Lil Trae pops another Perk 30 before he comes back to our sofa when Jay calls out "Shawtie, c'mere…"

I hesitate to get up and drag myself into our room and Jayceon shuts the door. "Yeah babe what's up?" I feel a little nervous because I don't know if Trae told him or if he's just mad because I'm not being excited about today's profits or if he found something else to argue about. Either way, I'm still on edge. I need a fucking pill or ah blunt to make this feeling fade away.

"How was yo' day? How'd our trap houses look today?" This isn't a good way for Jay to start off a conversation because it's unusual.

"Uhm, good, I went over to the South Side trap to get numbers and there was drama wit dis white bitch, her drug addict mom, and Ray-Ray…then Lil Trae was already over at tha East Side trap when…" before I could tell him the baby news and my disappointment he jumps in with a guilty face telling me that he's sorry. "Sorry fo' what baby?"

"Look, baby girl, I just wanted to letchu know dat I ain't been treatin' yo' right dese last few months. This all night paperchasin' and hustlin' got me on my grind and I been takin' dat frustration out on yo'…that's not cool. Shawtie I just wanted to say I ain't mean to hit chu the other night. It takes a big person to say they sorry and yo' know I ain't good at sayin' dat." He kisses the side of my neck and back up to my glossy lips when he adds "Daddy's sorry, so lemmie take yo' out fo' tha night and make it up the right way!" His hand glides over my thigh and we kiss for a few, but I'm not really feelin' his plan.

35

"Babe, I don't feel like-"

Pulling away he stands up from the bed ready to go back into the living room when he says, "Get ready and hop in tha whip, I don't wanna hear anotha muthafuckin' word, a'ight!"

I know it's about to be somewhere nice and fancy or a shopping spree. I think that's exactly what I need to get my mind off this loss, so fuck it, we can ball tonight and he can pay for his bullshit ways. I freshen up then Jay grabs my hand and leads me off to one of the suburbanite malls while Lil Trae stays faded on the couch nodding on and off. Twenty minutes and Jay's mashin' the gas because we're on the freeway with The Game banging in the system.

Footlocker is packed with kids running around and parents trying to agree on which pair to buy for spring. We step in and the museum sized basketball hoop hanging from the ceiling greets us. A friendly sales associate says "hi" to me and gives Jay the famous head nod. With stacks on deck I should be prepared to get more than three pairs but I'm not feeling it. I have to fake it for Jayceon. Hell maybe after popping a few tags then I'll get back to the old Chantell. Jay's already found a pair that he thinks I would look fly in, holding it up like a toy from one of those claw machines. "Ay, babe, look at dese!"

I nod my head, "yeah, they look a'ight..."

"Pssh, yo' don't like dese? They're tha Flight series and they got the black on red vibe..."

I spot the toddler shoes and wander over to them. I was picturing a pregnant me and Jayceon behind me helping pick out new shoes for our baby, the one we could have had... Now he's lost like a kid. When I snap out of my fantasy, my eyes start to tear up as I walk away and find Jay with two boxes beside him. "What kind yo' feelin' to get Jay?" He opens up both boxes and shows me some fresh ass J's. An all-black pair with a few designs of red and then a new pair of forces catch my attention.

"Pick yo' out somethin' mama..." He nudges me over to my section and I decided to get two pairs of Flight's one all Varsity Red and the other was a pair of all black forces, just like my boo. He pays the over friendly sales associate wearing glasses, not the same one we saw earlier or the other three circling the store for potential sales. We step out of there and I let Jay lead the way.

Next is Victoria Secrets, another favorite store of ours. Jayceon loves to keep my underwear drawer iced out with plenty of v-strings, thongs and panties. Enjoying the thought of helping me pick out which ones, we hold hands as we gallop in, Foot Locker bags trailing behind us. These prissy ass bitches in here cringe as soon as me and my babe find our way in and head straight to a sexy table with all the lacey v-strings I can see. Jay sets his bag on the floor beside us, posted up against the stand of this table and takes mine from me. We browse through the neon, animal print, and vibrant colors while Jayceon moves behind me, gripping my curves and kissing the back of my neck. "Ooh, shit look at those ma," he points to a purple v-string with animal print that's a sexy black and white.

"Mmhmm." Usually I'm more into this type of shopping but right now I don't feel like my usual confident, sexy self. Can Jayceon tell?

We make our way over to the sweat suits with the glitter sequence jackets and Jay lets me pick out five. That doubles my collection, so now I'm excited, my mood starts to drift back to the old me when Jay calls me over to a bra and panty set. Its rouge red with lace trim and my size. Jay licks his sexy lips and whispers "Yo' think yo' could rock dis mama?"

I bite my lip and turn my head, damn a nigga know how to make me blush. I purr back "mhmm, yeah Daddy…"

His hand cradles my neck when he gives me a sincere kiss and then tells me "yeah, yo' goin' let Daddy make it up to you all night in dis sexy ass shit? C'mon let's get up out chere!"

While we're walking over to the florescent bright counter I can feel these nosey ass white bitches hatin' and wonderin' how we got all dis paper on deck. I wanna scream at them from their blonde highlights to their pointy heels that yeah, we got shit on the low and my baby is on his hustlin' shit with the pills, dro, and now we've gotta lil coke. But now is not the place. A smirk and seein' Jayceon count all twenty's to the sales bitch will be sufficient.

We hit up one last store, the Coach Factory and he splurges on a new Coach purse. It's the Poppy Collection and I got the matching wallet. He throws in a few charms that hang off the outside strap and now we're off to get a bite to eat. I hope it's somewhere with reservations. "Chantell, yo' wanna eat here so we can hurry up and get home?" His eyes travel up and down my frame and I don't wanna upset the vibe with pouting about fast food.

"Uh, sure babe, yea what yo' feelin' to get?" He surveys the food court and spots a sub place called "Chris's Cheesesteaks" and tells me to hold down one of the flimsy tables. Our bags are piled up so high that I'm swimmin' in new gear and while Jayceon's gone I take a look around. Families from these nice ass neighborhoods sip on coffee drinks in white cups and kids play at the kid zone that looks like a space ship. Everyone is dressed similar with turtle necks, heavy coats with fake fur on the hoods and most wear glasses. Dangling earrings and fancy necklaces make them blend in together. Hell, Jayceon and I are the only ones who don't fit their mold. My tight ass Dior jeans and sexy Forever Twenty-One baby tee compliments my gold hoops with "J.M." etched in each one. I need to let Jay know that tomorrow I'm getting my hair fixed, because right now it's more than busted; it's horrible. Babe is still standing in line. He'll probably get us the same thing and two sweet teas. I try to shuffle our new gear around the table while I wonder if Jayceon could notice that I was tense tonight. Did he already hear my news about the miscarriage and try to drown my pain with plastic bags and twenty after twenty spent? Is that bitch really right about "abusive relationships?" Then again, what makes her qualified to judge me and my man? I need to call Dee up and tell her everything, or, if Jay leaves tomorrow which he probably will, I'll sneak her over and she can help me grieve. I swear to God, Jayceon needs to quit putting his hands on me like I'm one of dese hood rats. Tuh.

I see Jay weaving through the crowd of people, mugging a group of "wankstas" posted up by a fake plant. Our food smells good as hell; that blunt on the way over made me even hungrier. The sounds of people finding and deciding where to eat made us quiet at the table. The sky lights above us are dark from night's presence. "Ay, babe, yo' member when we used to go ova to dat mall when we first started datin'?" I smile and remember Jay pullin' up to my Auntie's house with the old school Cadillac on twenty-twos. Dee used to get so pissed because she knew Jayceon Michaels was a hustler and all about his money. We could fool Auntie for a while, long enough to let me get from the backseat to Jay's passengers seat.

"Yeah, Bae, I 'member dat shit!" We talk about sneaking out and smoking blunts off his friend's rooftop apartment over on South Clark Street by the park, and how we used to listen to that old school rap. My smiles end real quick when Jay changes the subject faster than a fiend can pop a pill.

Looking directly at me with his hat tilted to the side and his caramel face too serious, he asks "Fo' real though what's wrong withcha Shawtie?" I look at him like he's trippin' and try to deny his claim. "Chantell, why yo' ass lying? I'm finna give yo' one mo' time to gimmie a real answer…"

This is where I need to play it smart and tell Jayceon the real pain he's caused, the pain that I haven't buried yet with talks from Dee and four or five blunts with a few pills. "Babe, is this really the place? Whatcha think cuz yo' ass bought me some shit, I'm just goin' be on some Dr. Phil bullshit? Tuh!" I roll my eyes and cross my arms across my chest. Hell, my cheap ass food's probably cold now with all these stares and silent threats. Jayceon just sits there burning holes right through me. Chewing his food tense, he knows there's too many damn people to make a scene in this public spot. Inside my head I continue my tirade telling myself that this is how really I feel. Real talk, nigga fuck you! If you really cared you wouldn't have put me in this depressed mood anyway. Shit. That's what I wanna let him know but I know as well that now isn't the place to start that kind of argument. Instead I just sit there and let him wonder what's going through my head; I know how to play games too Jay, believe that.

After we keep mean muggin' each other for a solid twenty minutes the silent treatment becomes our only voice, I break down and decide to fill Jay in. A monotone voice that I muster up silently whispers to tell Jay "I had a miscarriage today." Tears whirl down my face and I lose control. Jayceon jumps up and holds me, moving my hands away from my face and lets me cry into his 4x airbrushed tee. I sob and sob so loud that Jay helps me up and we exit out the mall from the other side. He's carrying all of our new gear and I've got a cigarette lit, my hands too shaky to really care about the cold wind whipping by.

"Baby, why didn't you tell me when it happened? Huh? Yo' already know I would've been there to pick you up baby girl!" The protective side of Jayceon comes out like my black knight in shining armor with the heat beside his hip and I'm being rescued. We make it to the whip and he stores our stuff in the trunk. As we sit in the busy parking lot he gives me a much needed hug and I just cry and cry while he tells me "Shhh, it'll be okay mama. I'm goin' make it better tonight. Let Daddy fix dis issue we got mama...I swear to God I'm finna make it up baby!"

Jayceon puts the whip on autopilot as we pass all of our familiar settings and surrounds. The hos blend in with the stop signs and the crack heads merge in with the speed of how fast we drive to our local corner store. We hit this little liquor spot called "Jimmy's"-- at least that's what the locals call it-- and Jay puts it in park and leans over kissing my shoulder. "What yo' tryin' drank tonight mama?" His voice is soft like the rain that's starting to trickle down the windshield. "I don't care babe, whatever you want..." I face towards the window and just stare out blankly. I feel like this shit really can't be happening. When we get bottles it's to celebrate, not to console a loss, unless one of the homies gets shot or locked up. Jayceon goes inside. I can hear the "bing" of the convenient store bell and I light up another square. I picture Jay's face when I told him the bad news. A look of true sincere pain had shown through and the sorry that he told me was so true, so real, there's no way that the nurse knows my situation. The sorry and concern that Jay is showing isn't like the "sorry's" of the past from when he's fucked up and got caught or came home with a confession. No, not at all. The driver side door swings open and I kind of jumped due to being lost in my own thoughts. Holding up a Grey Goose bottle and another shorter bottle labeled Patron, I can tell he's ready to make up. "A'ight, so we goin' go back to the crib Daddy?" I ask tiredly, I pass him the square and he just starts driving.

"Nah Shawtie, we feelin' to hit up RedBox for a quick DVD and then we goin' go home and smash. Shit, you already know we 'bout to get it in!" A smirk quickly pops up on his face and before I know it we're home with two bottles and a movie.

I'm sitting in the car alone when I see Lil Trae come out the cut so I roll down my window. "What up?"

He shakes his head "Not shit, but cha boy bout to set shit off tonight!" He smiles at me and tells me he'll call before he comes over tomorrow, adding in "damn he got the candles lit and shit!" Wow, Jayceon ain't been this romantic since I don't know when, I guess I better get my ass in there and see what my baby's up to. See, my baby does know how to treat me like his street queen, main bitch, Shawtie and his true love. Fuck what these bitches say!

As I walk up the wooden stair case to our ghetto castle I can hear Pretty Ricky playing and Jayceon opens the door to a pitch black room with candles lit everywhere giving a loving and embracing vibe. I just stare with my mouth open admiring his romantic side and he invites me in. "Mrs. Michaels, welcome to your love trap house…" He hands me the newly lit blunt and damn it was fat too. Inhaling the good and exhaling the loss when he disappears in the bathroom, I hear the water running. Stripping down to my emotionally exhausted bare body I know that tonight, Jayceon Michaels, has not only my heart but my whole being. Mentally and emotionally, I know that Jay is here to make me feel good in all ways possible. "Grind On Me" keeps playing on repeat as we make our way into the shower. The water pours down onto us and he starts to rub my shoulders, getting me nice and relaxed. I'm curious why Jayceon is giving me all of this attention. Not that I don't appreciate it, but there aren't many days like there was a few years ago. Kissing my neck he whispers "What's on yo' mind Shawtie?"

I turn around and move my palms up and down his chest, watching the water run down his skin when I tell him "Nothing…just trying to figure out why yo' ass is being so romantic and nice all of ah sudden…"

He picks me up and has my bare back against the shower wall, kissing from my lips to my fruit cups he says "It feels nice to be loved, and lately I ain't been doin' that. I just wanted to say I was sorry 'bout the other night and wanted to show that you're still my main bitch. You'll

always be my Shawtie and no one can ever take yo' fucking place ma!"
I watch him kiss on my breast as the water droplets dodge past him.

"That's really nice Jayceon, damn, yo' do know how to make ah
bitch feel special and important. I love you with all my muthafuckin'
heart babe. Do you love me the same?"

Moving back up, the steam from the shower gets more intense and
so does his stare. He finally whispers after a short kiss "Yeah babe,
I'm finna always love you with all my muthafuckin' heart!" We finish
rinsing off and he orders me to get my ass in the living room. Towels
still wrapped around us, we walk into the kitchen. He sets out two shot
glasses. He pours two shots of Patron in the neon ones we got from
Virginia Beach. Before we toast and celebrate, I pause for a brief moment to think about the baby, well, the baby that we could have had.
It makes me take the shot quicker to drench the pain and make me
numb, plus Patron makes sex so much better for us. Jayceon keeps
talking about how we're going to be out the hood someday and soon
I can be baby mom's status and wifey too. But all I can hear is my own
thoughts replaying into more detail about what happened earlier with
Trae and seeing Jayceon's real reaction.

He says he can't wait to make our dreams come true and we both
take a shot. He pours another round and we toast to great make-up
sex. Jayceon takes one more shot by himself and says cheers to my slip
and slide wet pussy, because after this shot, its finna get murked. A
huge cheesy grin slides across his face and he starts to lick his lips. I
already know I'm in trouble when he picks my ass up and carries me
over to the couch. Getting on his knees after he tries his best to set me
gently onto the couch, he asks me if I'm ready. "Ready for what? Yo' to
eat this…" I start playing with it and he keeps staring from my hand
toying with it back to my face.

"Nah, Shawtie, is yo' ready for me to make yo' call me Daddy all
night?!" Moving my legs their separate ways he gets a taste, a few licks
up and down and stops; he just stares at me.

I open my eyes. He's already got me thrusting up and down going
with his motion, and I just stare at him "Why yo' stop babe?" I beg him,
"Mmhmm, finish eating me out…"

Looking up at me from in-between my thighs with that hypnotizing stare, he commands me "Call me Daddy." That shit turns both of us on, especially after a few shots. Before he even takes one more lick, I scream out what he loves to hear. He pulls me closer and dives right in, sucking, slurping and finger fucking me until I bust, twice. He licks off his index finger and has me lick off his middle finger, I swirl my tongue around it.

"Mmhmm, whatcha got next Daddy?" Jay tells me to get up and come over here, but as soon as I get by the end of the couch, he turns around and pushes me over the arm of the couch, I just laugh and squeal with delightment. "Ohh, shit, Jayceon, whatcha 'bout to start doin'-" His palm smacks my ass firmly and I yelp out a little, some of it was from the surprise of not being able to see what's next and a little bit was from the sting.

Jayceon gives me a few more hits before he asks me "Whose ass is dis? Huh?!" I yell back that it's Jayceon Michael's, and he smacks me even harder.

"Ahh, shit, why yo' smack me so damn hard?"

I could feel his hand raise up in the air when he asks me again, "I said whose ass is this?" See when Jayceon gets tipsy or drunk he's overly aggressive, so to him, he needs to hear only one answer: *Daddy*. Any other answer will result in a smack, a slap, getting dick'd down or another round of head. Sometimes, it's all of those. I cry out that its Daddy's, all his and he backs off, letting me get up. "C'mon mama I'm finna fuck yo' all over dis apartment tonight!" His kisses guide us back to where we started in the bathroom. My mouth meets his excited dick and we get tangled up in kissing and I give him head, from the shower to the bathroom counter, and back over to the couch. Next is the kitchen counter with a few missionary strokes and then the bedroom.

Its four and a half hours later, a hot shower, great head, 69 and six shots of Patron. Jay guzzled the rest of our Grey Goose and got more than loose doing all those freaky things we both like. Damn, a nigga got me sprung.

Chapter Eight

The ceiling fan just stares back and all I can think about is these past few days. Last night was more than amazing. It was one of the best nights we've had in a while but I wish that it didn't have to happen, due to our loss. It does show me that Jayceon really does have true love for me. I can still hear the sound of his voice when he called me "Mrs. Michaels." It made me feel like nothing could touch me or hurt us. I knew right then that Lil Trae was right, he might be ready to really settle down and put a rock on my wedding finger, and not on the street's hand. Shit, just the wonderful feeling of his love last night, caressing, and tongue lashings, felt amazing and reassuring. I know that babe would do anything for me. Shit, the Foot Locker bags and new Coach Purses show it and the candles with endless rounds of love making prove it. I remember how Jayceon used to really be in these streets trying to work his way up to boss status from jacking the cars, hitting licks on houses and Pawn Shops, so I shouldn't trip when all he has to do is check on a trap here and there. I need to put myself in check. Jayceon rolled over and cuddled up to the comforter. I wiped my eyes to get the sleepiness out and just laid there thinking. If I wouldn't have started the argument that night by popping off with my smart-ass mouth maybe I could feel the baby's kick in a few months. Or if I wouldn't have popped that late night pill maybe we'd be choosing baby names, well if it was a girl. If we would have found out it was a boy it would automatically be a Jr. No doubt about it. I toss and turn a little, just having these thoughts flood through my mind, the thoughts that led up to the ER visit and Lil Trae being my shofar to find the devastating facts. I need to heal and get over it, and I'm sure time will help, but right now I swear I feel so fucking guilty. Rolling over Jayceon wakes up and kisses my naked chest staring at me the whole time. Last night's Patron bottle glows all glass and almost no liquor from the afternoon's sunshine rays and the ashtray is littered with roaches. Moving back up to face me Jayceon whispers in my ear when he sounds just like Young Jeezy saying "Babe, I think we need ah vacation!" My eyes get wide with disbelief, we haven't left the state since our Virginia Beach trip! "What! Where to boo?!" I sound like a six year old getting ready to find out that their rich parents are taking them to Disney World with all the princess and magical bullshit. Jayceon laughs and I climb on top when he announces "Whatcha think 'bout Florida Keys lil mama?" We kiss and he grips my fat ass as we start to grind a little when he smacks my ass and makes me get off. I can tell he wants to start his day and get it rolling, I'm sure we've got a lot to do if we're really leaving. Walking over to the safe he punches in the code and it pops open when he counts out some money. Handing me four stacks he smiles and says "We goin' need some mo' gear so while Daddy's out in dese streets go cop some new shit mama." Kissing me back onto the bed I feel like we're 'bout to start what we ended last night when he tells me to get some more Ecko shorts and wife beats for him. I tuck the stacks in my brand new purse and zip it up when I let Jayceon know "okay Daddy, yo' already know we goin' stay fresh to death!"

After forty five minutes of getting ready with a shower, fixing my hair up as best as I can and throwin' some eyeshaddow and mascara on I go see what Jay's doing in the kitchen. "Hey babe, do you care if someone goes with me while I shop for us...you know I hate going alone..." He tells me that Lil Trae is over at the South Side trap and he's about to go meet up with him. They've got to go check on the East Side trap together and go handle some other business before we leave so he offered to see if Killa Kam is busy. The two way chirps and Killa

Kam is just chillin' over at his side bitch's crib, but we all know it's his main bitch. See ever since his old lady left him about a year ago he's been sweatin' this trick. We all tease him about it because he doesn't call her his "boo" or his "baby" just his "side bitch" anytime someone's over, even in-front of her face, so we clown on him super hard. We all know the truth and so does that two dollar trick. Its set-up Killa Kam is on his way and Jayceon leaves out the door with a sweet kiss. I change to a sexy push up bra and the matching panties, I wonder what it's like to be Jayceon Michaels for the day.

Chapter Nine

All of the lonely nights with Jay away at the trap or fuckin' with some hood rat bitch has had me beyond bitter and I think it's time that I see what it's like to play like a hustler for the day. Since my cheating record doesn't exist I might as well get a one night stand in before we tie the knot someday. By the way Trae talks it will be soon, so as I get ready for the day, I let the past sweep in and light another roach from last night. Four knocks at the door lets me know its Kam and I grab my bag and go get the door. "Ay what's good?" Killa Kam gives me dap and asks if I'm ready to go. A big smile across my face would give the neighbor an impression that it's a first date when we get in his pimped out candy apple red Dodge Durango and hit the mall. Kam turns down the system to take a business call and I just stare out the window. I remember when I would hear from these fiends and the streets that Jay was busy makin' us money and while doing that he was fucking with this trick named Tammie. Then there was Theresa and that freak from club June Bug named Lacey. Those are the hos that I know of, not to mention when Trae pulled me to the side at a super bowl party to let me know that bitch across the room, yeah Jay fucked her too. I think her name was T'wana or Tameka; hell after a while they all blend in. That was in a two or three year span but it still feels the same, just like yesterday. I can remember smelling the perfume and I've found lip gloss or lip stick stains that I don't even rock, so yeah I've caught a nigga cheating. Do you even know how many times I've had to change my number because hos would steady be calling trying to act like their the real Mrs. Michaels, but we all know who that really is. Yup, it's me and I let all these side hos know…Jayceon Michaels is mine. Forever, through the hood times to penthouse hotel rooms and Dayton rims sitting on a candy coated ride. Escalade, 300, Bens and Cadillacs I've been there since we've been teenagers up to now and I don't plan to leave! We park by a Best Buy a few blocks from the mall and Kam parks the Durango. "Shawtie, lemmie roll dis blunt and smoke dis, then I need to go in Best Buy to grab a new case and charger. I hate this damn piece of shit case I got." We pass the joint and laugh at all of the nerds that pass by the whip. Some carry a bag probably full of video games or movies while some gleam with a new game system under their arm like a hot date or like my Coach bag. What lames! We finish up the 'dro and make our way inside the tech store, surrounding ourselves in tons of fun merchandise. "Ooh Kam look at dat big ass T.V. shit Jayceon would love dat!" We "ooh" and "ahh" at other shit and make our way to the phone section. Killa Kam is flirting with some sales associate in her all blue uniform shirt and tight ass khaki pants. Glasses and stick thin straight hair make her blend into this place, she looks like a girl on one of their flyers for a door buster sale. I hear him tell her "yeah, I do need a new phone…cha you know, if you don't gotta man…" and I just roll my eyes. I go walk over to the CDs and see who's popping in the Rap section. I find some Haystak, Game, Busta and of course Tupac. Eminem and Jay-Z are there with Mary J. and Monica. Damn. I really want to buy some CDs to play on the way to Florida. I know that music is free now-a-days but there's nothing like copin' a CD and checkin' out the album art, cover and having the CD as yours. I still remember trading CDs and having them in those huge cases with the plastic covers to protect them. I grab a few classics and decide to go see what Kam's up to. A new blonde haired bitch is over by Kam; she looks like the manager. He's looking at new phones. Waving me over, he must want my opinion. "Ay Chantell, whatcha think 'bout dis phone?" It's the HTC Evo 4G.

"Shit, it's nice as fuck, yo' goin' cop it?" He can't make his mind up; it is a sweet ass phone. "Brah, you should get it...ooh, look at that IPhone!" Killa Kam goes back and forth, he finally picks the EVO and we get out of there with some paper work done, with three hundred and fifty bucks gone. He got a new phone, sweet case with a holster clip, and the first chick's number. We get back in the whip and I ask him with a little bit of jealousy "Yo' you goin' ask Shawtie out?"

He just laughs and says "hell nah, that bitch got played!" Now I'm lost because he was really acting like he was digging her. He carries on while we find a spot at the mall and says "Shawtie gave me an employee discount...so I gave her fifty and her manager gave her the override code!" I just shake my head, I don't believe his ass.

"Lemmie see dat muthafuckin' receipt cuz there ain't no way she gave you dat cheep of ah discount nigga!"

He exclaims "Nah there wasn't no receipt, I talked her into it because I went to High School with her older brother James. You know Lil Jim? Her younger brother was that lil dude they used to call Pringles because his fat ass always eatin' some chips or some type of snack shit...Yeah we used to be real tight before I got set-up with Jayceon. So, she gave me his number for a new connect and shit and helped me out...damn it's a small world!"

The white manila faces all look the same from the last time me and Jay were here popping tags. We roll over to the Marc Ecko store so I can cop Jayceon some new gear while Killa Kam is my escort for the day, and he doesn't know but soon to be one night stand if the rush lingers between us. I get Jayceon ten pairs of shorts, five polo shirts and a few tee shirts with tight designs before we hit the next store. Killa Kam strolls right beside me on some boo type shit, but he's still window shopping on these fancy broads. Carrying an arm full of bags already we hit a few more stores. Next is Vickie C's because I want to look sexy for Jay and also to see if Killa Kam has any chemistry in here with me, just to see if my idea would work. I go to a table with colorful thongs in every pattern imaginable and pick one out. Holding it out I ask Kam "do you think I would look sexy in this?" I give him a smug look with a sexy smirk and he just nods his head. He probably doesn't know how to take my question, being that I am Jayceon's main bitch.

"Uh, yeah, fo' sho…" and he trails off. But by the time we leave there, I've got him helping me pick a few things out and when we're at the checkout counter with one of those fake bitches hatin; he stands proud beside me and our hands collide to see who's going to grab the pink bag first. I felt a shock wave of irresistible sensation go through me and by the look on Kam's face I can tell he knows what I'm thinking. As we walk a few stores down he walks closer like he's almost claiming me. He tells me how sexy I would look in that lacey black bra and pantie set. "Yeah, you think so?" is all I say and he just smiles. We hit a few more stores; some of them we just window shop in. By the end of the day I've spent close to two stacks, which is only half of the bank that Jay gave me. It's probably around five or six because the sun is starting to set when Killa Kam asks if I'm hungry. "Yeah, I'm light weight hungry…whatchu feel like eatin?"

We start naming off restaurants around here some fast food and others a little more special when he suggests "I ain't neva been to the Melting Pot…" I glance over at him, shit I've neva heard of that.

"What's that?" I ask with a little curiosity.

"Oh, well, its dis sweet ass place where you eat off sticks, I mean skewers." We both laugh. "Yeah, there's like cheese with food, like bread and meat and then there's a chocolate desert one too."

I reply "Damn, that sounds fancy as fuck. You know how to get there?" Nodding his head we throw Jay's new gear in the back of Killa Kam's whip and we're off to dinner. Hopefully I get a better desert than melted chocolate with strawberries!

"Welcome to the Melting Pot! How many for your party tonight?" A nice hostess asks as we step inside. Killa Kam speaks up and says "two" and she sits us at a booth near a window in the front. As we approach the table she asks, "Is a window seat fine?" We both say yes and she says our waitress will be over to get us drinks in a few. We both marvel about how nice this place is and we just stare around for the first five minutes. We sit across from each other. They have candles at each table and the place is packed.

"Wow, I'm surprised dat we gotta table in here…"

Killa Kam adds "Yeah, me too…" He gives me a smile that he saves for all the hos and future hook-ups. We order drinks and the curly haired waitress named Alicia gives us each a menu, explaining a little history and the best choice for us to start off with. Going to the bar to retrieve our drinks we sit in silence for a moment. He's staring dead at me and I'm mugging back. Is he looking at me like just a one night stand or the type of chick that he'd want to wife? The atmosphere is sexy and grown, almost like a club that serves food. Alicia brings us our drinks back before we can ask each other what we're really think-ing. Killa Kam got a Budweiser and I chose a cocktail called the Love Martini. It's their signature drink and after the chemistry in Vicki C's I'm ready to see if it will work.

Alicia shows us our options for dinner and we go with the four course experience, she then informs us "The four course includes a cheese fondue, individual salads, individual entrée's and as for des-sert, a chocolate fondue. Let's start off with the first course. What type of cheese fondue would you like?" We both stare at our choices and Killa Kam picks the cheddar. She lets us know that salads are next and I pick a caesar salad while Kam gets the house salad. We both agree on The Classic choice for the entrée and dessert is dark chocolate fon-due. I hope it's more than pound cake and strawberries! Sipping my Love Martini slowly I can taste the Peach Schnapps; it makes me lick my lips so lustfully. Asking Kam how he found out about this place I'm wondering why Jayceon hasn't taken me here yet?

"Aww, well when me and my ex were together I took her here every year for Valentine's Day and a few times throughout the year just to show some love…"

All I can say "Aww that's sweet…I bet you miss her huh?" He auto-matically puts up a street front when he chimes in "nah, I don't miss that bitch, she wasn't no ride-or-die type bitch so she had to get cut… plus it was just the small things that she couldn't do for me." I nod my head and he continues "Like you know how when Jay's away at the trap or where eva that you understand why he's gone. There's a reason. You don't blow his phone up all the time because you're lonely or is tryin' to distract him from tha Game you know…where Tiff just kept callin', causin' fights and makin' childish ass scenes. And I just wasn't feelin' that wit lil mama. She didn't know how to be a street soldier, so I had to just let go…"

Now I feel like we're on Maury when I ask him "Well, do you still got love for Tiff?" He quickly says "Hell nah, I don't love these hos!" Our first course comes out with melted cheddar cheese that's a mix of beer and other ingredients. A variety of things to dip in it like bread and other toppings are ready for us to slam on. Alicia gets Killa Kam another beer and I opt for just a plain Coke while we start to dig in. The thoughts of back in the day are coming in my mind strong. See, right when I met Jayceon I had met Kam too. They were really tight and honestly I just wanted not only a hood dude to be my boo but I also wanted someone who was a true soldier. Jay and Kam were both that. I met Jay first so I built up a crush on him and the rest is history. Not too long after that Kam met Tiff at a party that we all went to. Sometimes when Jay's away in the streets I think to myself what if I would've picked Kam instead of Jayceon? Both hustle and grind, both have street credit, but now that we're older Jay just has a little more paper and power. But, sometimes I think is all that extra really worth Jay's cheatin' ass ways and negative compliments mixed with fist fights? Kam hardly hit Tiff and if he did it was because she went off on the fucking deep end. Anyways, it's been in my mind for quite sometime to see if Kam and I really even had a spark or if it was just a fantasy of mine. I hope I can play my cards right and fulfill my darkest desire.

Killa Kam catches me off guard when he asks me "Whatchu bein' all quiet fo' Shawtie?"

I daze back in and say "Oh, nothin'…just wonderin' 'bout shit that I can't change."

Kam starts to pry into my thoughts when he brings up the fight with Jay from a few days ago. "When you and Jayceon fight, like real talk fight, is it because you start it and he just finishes it or does he go off the deep end?" Before I can answer the waitress interrupts with more drinks and I start to answer when Kam mentions "Yeah, I see how he be doin' niggas at the Trap if they don't make the money flow or if they try and steal a pill or two…Jayceon has a short fuse fo' real…"

I say "Yeah, he does have anger issues, I think, but that's just how he was raised you know. Shit, me and Dee were on the same type of shit too, I guess it just depends. The last fight I started because I was accusing' him of shit when he got home, and questioning him about why it took so long to come back home…" Listening closely Kam lets me keep talking "It went from some ho calling my phone, to him not getting in until the next day and then next thing I know I'm against a wall. Lil Trae came over and Jay sent me to our room, a few words were said, a few hits got thrown out and I took a shower and went to sleep… We had great make-up sex but sometimes, I'm sick of the making-up and breaking-up shit, you know?"

Dipping a piece of sourdough bread into the cheese Kam says "Yeah, me and Tiff was on that same bullshit…I know personally I need to find someone who ain't on that type of shit all the time. It's not bad every once in a while, but that constant cycle, yeah it really does damage…If I was you, I would try to let Jay know how you really feel!" Telling Killa Kam that it wouldn't matter what I tell Jay, our next course comes out.

Salads are amazing. My caesar is crunchy and crisp the dressing is delicious. Killa Kam lets me take a bite of his house salad off of his fork. I feel like we're a new couple as I glide the food off the fork. I give him such a sexy stare. I think the Love Martini is working; can he notice it too? Our third course comes out and I'm getting full, Kam is still eating and trying to dip everything he can in the Gorgonzola port sauce. Angus Sirloin, shrimp, chicken and pork medallion all accompany the third course but I can't wait for the fourth course, the chocolate. Swirling the dark chocolate around Killa Kam lets me know "If you was my main Shawtie, or any chick that's a dedicated ride-or-die, I wouldn't do ya like that…" He just won't let this go. It's like he has to prove to me, that if I was his, shit would definitely be different. I find it exciting, attractive even, that someone would want to try and change my view of life. From a different relationship, different love, hell, even different fights it makes me stare deep into his eyes. I catch that spark of a connection that I've been wanting for all these years. Dipping a strawberry I held it over the table while Kam takes a bite. Licking his lips he reaches for my hand across the table, grazing my fingers and we lock hands. The flame is lit between us. He tells the waitress to give us each a glass of Amaretto Disaronno on the rocks. He feeds me a strawberry too, then a banana and I give him a taste of chocolate from my middle finger. He nibbles at my finger and before I can move my hand back he sucks my finger and swirls his tongue around it. Alicia interrupts our freaky vibe by setting the drinks on the rocks beside each of us. Asking us if we needed anything else, neither one of us looks away from the other as we say "no." Damn, this nigga has my pussy super wet like a rain storm. He gives my finger back, opening his mouth slightly and I let a soft moan slip out. Catching myself I bite my lower lip. "Yeah, you like dat Shawtie?" I don't give any other signals of how sprung I truly am because for a brief second I feel guilty about cheating. This isn't who Chantell Saunders soon-to-be Michaels acts. I don't cheat, yeah I've fantasized by myself but never took it past that… He licks his lips and takes his hand away from mine. Swirling his finger in the hot dark chocolate he lets me get a taste. I pretend it's more than a finger when I suck all of the sweet treat off, his eyes get real narrow and I can tell a nigga is sprung. We finish up desert in here and head back to the car, walking side-by-side like a newly established couple. Laughing to the car, Killa Kam opens my door and hops in too. Blaring the system we have another blunt in rotation and he asks what's next. I can see his large package bulge through his light denim Girbaud jeans. Smiling at his jeans it's getting late and we start to pull away from the mall when Jayceon calls.

"Oh shit, it's Jay!" I act surprised like I forgot that I even had a man.

"Answer it Shawtie, tell him we still got some shopping to do…"

I add to the lie "yeah and I'll say I'm spendin' the night at Dee's so you can drop me off and she can finish up the shopping spree with me…he'll believe dat."

"Hi baby!" I say overly chirpy.

"What's good baby girl…where you at mama?"

"Oh, we still hittin' dese outlet malls…where you at baby?"

He tells me he's still ridin' 'round with Trae getting shit ready for our leave of absence from the streets.

"Oh, okay boo, well since yo' still in the streets can I stay with Dee for the night? We've been wantin' to kick it and plus I need to tell her where we goin' and shit."

Pausing from our call he gives Trae a few trap numbers when he asks me what I said. I repeat it to him and he gives me the approval.

"Where's Killa Kam at?" I tell him he's 'bout to drop me off. A big grin slides over Kam's face as he silently sits there hitting the 'dro.

"A'ight baby just call me when you get to Dee's and when ya'll leave her crib tomorrow, a'ight?!" I tell him okay as always, and we hang up with a kiss over the phone. I put the phone back in the new Coach purse Jayceon got me and set it on Kam's floor board.

Putting the L in rotation he asks "So, where you feelin' to go now girl?"

I can see he's wonderin' if I'm gonna take it there so I offer "You wanna get a room at the 'telly? We can go to the Hilton or Marriott… if you're down for that Kam…"

He starts to think about it, I can see his wheels turning. This is one of his main nigga's chicks, not just any chick but a wifey type bitch. Deep down he knew that one of the reasons Tiff left was due to an incident with Jay. Fuck it, why not? Payback's always a bitch when he says to me "C'mon Shawtie lets go hit the corner store and check in at the Hilton!"

The wheels spin as we talk mad shit about Jayceon. Kam starts it off, I think to end the silence between us. He turns down the system and asks "So, Shawtie why yo' goin choose me fo' da nite?"

I just stare at all of the festive lights that make up a part of the malls outside appearance. "Well, I don't know…" I let him wonder for a minute, see what he's going to say back.

"Yo' don't know…shit, I could tell you've been wantin' to chance a nigga from day one, way back in the day!" I try and laugh to cover the truth up and start to deny it. Screamin' over top of my false claims, he knows he's gotta bitch sprung when he says "Shit, why yo' frontin'…I can tell when a female is diggin' me and I know Jay's gotta see it too…

Speakin' of dat nigga, he really ain't treatin' yo' ass right the way you should be. You know mama, shouldn't no dude put his hands on you, I bet you and Dee been talkin 'bout that shit for days huh?"

He's got me pegged but I can't let him know. "Nah, see Jay usually don't-"

"Usually don't…that's not a good excuse." I know he's dead ass right so I just turn up the volume on his deck and he smiles. He knows he's got me on this one. We stop at a little liquor spot and he asks me what I want to drink. I told him to get some Patron; he said he didn't like that.

I said, "Well fine, get a bottle for me and one for you, big spender."

He just shook his head and played the game he does to most bitches "you'll be happy wit whateva I get cha' Shawtie…" I smile and keep on the lookout for Jayceon or one of his nosey ass partna's in case they on the lookout. Not too long later Kam comes out of the fancy liquor store with two brown paper bags. One for me and one for him. Oh shit, a nigga really do care! We drive over to the Hilton Palmer House off of East Monroe Street his hand sways in-between my thighs and the conversation is drowned out with the system bangin'. We stay flirtin' till we pull up and Killa Kam hops out into the telly.

"Yeah, I need a king bed suite, what room's ya'll got available?" The hotel receptionist picks at the keys on her keyboard, her auburn ponytail shines with the florescent lighting.

"Sir, it looks like we have a few different rooms available. The one that would best suite you and her would probably be our Romance Package. It includes a king bed, two bathrooms on the executive floor. That room would be $313.12 for the night with taxes included."

Scrolling down the page Kam interrupts her. "Is that the best room you have for tonight?"

"Let me check sir."

I wait in the car with the bottles and watch all the turtle neck wearing white folks flock inside to the warm heat. Taking a deep breath I actually say out loud to myself "I can't believe I'm going to cheat! Oh shit, if Jay ever found out…I would be in the hood's newsletter for wifey missing...I've gotta call Dee! I start to dial her number when Killa Kam sways through the entrance and hops in the whip.

"Who you callin' Shawtie?" He looks concerned like I've changed my mind and called Jayceon to stop this from happening.

I lie and say "No one, I was checking the time."

He keeps his eye on me and says "A'ight lil' mama we gotta room and I'm bout to have dude valet park dis bitch." Grabbing his stash of weed and a brick of coke out the glove box we threw it in one of my Vickie C's bags. I question him about the heat under the seat. "Oh, nah I ain't worried 'bout that. Grabbing it from under the seat and trying to keep it out of plain view he stuffs it in his waist band of his jeans. "There, we all set Shawtie?" I just laugh and get out the whip. Kam points the dressed up bellman to his ride and leaves him a tip. I think I saw a fifty, or was it two that slid out from his pocket?

Acting like we're a couple, he lets me strut in front and we fast walk to the hotel's elevator. No one is waiting for the doors to open and Kam snatches the all pink bag from me. To not cause a scene he starts to role play. "Here babe, lemmie hold dat for you. You're a princess, can't have yo' carrying' nothin'!" A few onlookers glance our way and the elevator chirps as we step aside, a crew of grey haired folks step off. We give them a fake smile and we've got the all gold elevator to ourselves. Peeping out of the corner of my eye I catch him mugging me up and down and I lick my lips back at him. He gives me a small kiss and we're on the fourth floor. Room 408 here we come!

Killa Kam slides in the room key card like he's trying to get his hands down my pants and we're inside a sweet ass suite. Rose petals lay on the floor trailing to an all-white bedspread with black embroidery. Huge oversized pillows stare back and we hurry up and get inside; we're as giddy as a third date couple. "Damn, nigga, look at chu...I see you!" I'm not goin' lie this nigga went all out, damn...The Vickie C's bag gets set down on the entertainment stand and Kam takes his shirt off. Washboard abs greet my sight and the heat is still on him. Damn, Killa Kam looks so fuckin' fine!

Unbuckling his belt but still leaving it in the loops he tells me in his sexy ass hustler voice to "c'mere sexy..." I follow his words laced with lust and he French kisses me. Noticing my tongue ring personally, he takes off my shirt while we kiss. Slick move. Biting my lip he kisses from my glossed out lips to my neck and playfully flicks his tongue at my earlobe.

"Mmhmm, oh shit, Kam." I already feel lost in a fantasy. Is this fo' real?! Picking me up he takes me over to the bathroom's marble double sink and my thighs open right up. Rubbing up and down and in-between 'em he kisses even more passionately.

"Yo' tryin' hop in the shower Chantell?" I can't even talk in this whirlwind of sin. All I can do is cling on to him while he kisses and licks, and as I start to scratch his back.

"Ohh, shit, yo' ah lil freak huh? I can't wait to hear that sexy ass moan." Killa Kam says as his jeans fall to the floor while he let his grip go. He already put the heat by the bag in the other room. Boxers show a swollen package in the middle and I can tell he isn't small. This nigga has to be every bit of nine inches, maybe ten. I get undressed while he turns the water on and rain drops fall straight from the ceiling. Steam starts to cling to the bathroom mirror as we step inside. Calmly massaging my shoulders he tells me "Damn boo you're fucking tense!"

I just moan with a sigh and let him continue rubbing, after a few minutes all I can do is shake my head and say "Yeah, I know…I've been going through some shit lately…"

Killa Kam kisses on the back of my neck a deep passionate kiss when he whispers "I can fix dat fo' you if yo' let me." I turn around to face him and work my way from his tatted up chest down to his huge dick and start to give him a hand job. He must know that I'm impressed because he lets me know "Yeah, count the inches, there's ten and ah half, can that reach up in yo' ribs?" I just have a cheesy smile as I finished getting on my knees. Hot water pours down on us as I start to give him head. His toes start to curl and I can hear his muffled moans while he grabs a fistful of hair, helping me go down further and further each time. Right before he busts he pulls my lips off his chap stick and we both move back over to the bathroom counter as he bends me over, inspecting my goodies. Tellin' me how tight my pussy is, I know that he can tell I only let Jay play in my river, ain't no other niggas, well, except Kam now. I don't want fucked against the counter, not on the first round, so we move over to the rose pedal bed and get it popping. Round one lasts longer than I thought and wasn't as rough like the way me and Jay fuck. Killa Kam took his time when he laid me down, a real gentlemen when he ate the kitty, slow stroked from the front and fast from the back. We took a rest before the next round and partied with a few rounds of shots. Another blunt got lit on the balcony and by now Jayceon was away from my thoughts. Me and Killa Kam fucked all night; we both busted so many nuts I lost count. The new day and sun rise was seen from me peeking up from doggy-style, Kam smashing. We finally fell asleep around five or six I think.

I laid awake for a good twenty minutes before I realized that this wasn't a dream. I was in a nice ass Hilton hotel with Killa Kam, one of my all-time fantasies. Where the hell is he at? What side of town are we on again and why does my head hurt this damn much? I roll over and try to gather my surroundings. I see Kam's phone sitting on the night stand beside the bottles we killed last night. His keys aren't in my sleepy sight. I hope a nigga didn't leave me here, that'd be all bad! Pulling the sheets back, my thighs and pussy still feel wet and sticky. I sit up and just take in the beauty of the balcony, the hotel suite and I finally decide to throw on my sweatpants and an Ecko wife beat. I lit up a roach left in last night's ashtray. Taking in the early morning sun light I cuddle up in my hoodie and start to curse at the cold ass weather when I hear the sliding glass door open.

"What's good Shawtie?" It's Kam and he's got a fresh fit for me and a twenty ounce mountain dew.

Grabbing my chest "I'm glad yo' ass ain't Jay, tha muthafuckin' police or room service cuz yo' slick ass snuck up on me!" He just smiles and we're in a quick rotation.

I offer to blaze one more L when he lets me know "Nah, we gotta bounce cuz room service comes in after check out, which is at noon, I think." We head back inside and he looks so hood just standing there with his sexy ass jeans, all black belt, fresh forces and no shirt on. I give him that look, he knows what I want, shit I was bad last night and I've gotta lie to Jay later so why not one more quickie. We take it to the shower from kisses to him getting head and slapping my ass while he strokes all ten inches in my favorite position. Deep down, I have the urge to go ahead and call him "Daddy" but that would signify that my goodies are his. That can't happen, I'm still in love with Jayceon Michaels, so I just think the shit really loud in my mind while he gives me one more taste on the bed.

"Shit, Shawtie, yo' got that bomb pussy, no wonder Jay keeps tabs on dat ass!" Wiping off his face and licking his lips, I just smile, I knew he was right. We go and get ready for the day with both of us rockin' a new outfit. He sports a new snapback hat, Mark Ecko jeans and a fresh airbrushed baggy tee. I'm stepin' out fresh in one of my new Vicky C's Pink Collection jumpsuits, my Coach purse matches perfect as I start to get a guilty conscience; we're just now pulling away from the parking lot.

"Dee, what's good bitch?" I call Dee while we're just wasting time driving around to get my alibi straight.

"Sup mama? Yo' ass up earlier than usual...Jay give yo' some morning dick?" She just laughs when I make her realize how serious I am.

"Nah Dee, look, has Jay called you in the last day...? Cuz I was out and shit but he don't know. I used yo' ass as an alibi sayin' I was going to spend the night with you and we'd finish shopping today for our Florida trip."

"Yo' what?! When ya'll going to Florida, for what? And are you fucking serious right now...Chantell...Jayceon called me last night at around one and I told him I ain't heard from yo'!" My heart drops like the blue lights were behind Kams car with a trunk full of work.

"Fuck!" "Fuck!" "Fuck!" Is all I can say out loud when Killa Kam pulls up to the drive-thru window. While he orders at Burger King I've got more issues than deciding what I want for breakfast, shit, and the way today's going I might as well hide. I have nowhere to hide from Jay. He knows where all my people live and all his main niggas would be on the hunt too. Oh my God! How could I be Jayceon Michaels main bitch and forget to cover my ass while being on some shady type shit?! The cashier at the window gives Killa Kam a cheesy smile. He's a lady's mayne, and he gives a hustler's laugh while collecting the change from his one hundred dollar bill.

Whining into the phone I asked Dee what I should do. She says "Girl, yo' really goin' get that ass in trouble, he probably goin' think you creepin' and if yo' ass thought ya'lls last fight a few nights ago was bad…oh shit…nigga goin' bring da heat!" She starts laughing when Kam hands me some hash browns as we park and eat. Now I'm pissed at Dee. Why the fuck would she just sit there and laugh? She's supposed to be my sister and shit and help me out!

"Dee, fo' real Jay really called?" I try to act like maybe if I didn't hear her right the first time; she'll just say this is a joke.

"Bitch, who's always got cha' back? Huh! Yeah Jayceon called and I told him you was over here passed out. He asked if you went shopping when he told me about ya'lls lil Florida trip and I lied. I told him yo' ass popped so many tags you ass couldn't even carry all the bags in and I'd have you back at the trap tomorrow once we got ready and shit. Yo' know yo' bitch gotcha covered!" I just thanked God when she says "That's what family is fo' lil sis, right?" I want to cry tears of joy, Jayceon won't know and my face won't get fucked up or worse. I munch on the breakfast sandwich when I tell her I'm finna get off here and let her know.

"I'ma call Jay now and tell him that Kam stopped over to kick it so since yo' ass had work he's goin' take me back home." She just shrugs and knows that I've got company. She'll get the details of last night later. We finish breakfast and we're off to hit a few more stores. I've really gotta play the shop 'til yo' drop card so that means Jayceon needs more gear. We hit a few more stores to get some wife beats, Ecko boxers with the graffiti, and I bought Jayceon a new pair of stunna shades. It's almost one by the time my phone rings with me and Jay's picture across the screen.

"Dee, turn that shit down boo…Hi baby!" I'm playing into this shit.

"Ay mama what's up? Where yo' and Dee at?" I let him know that we're still shopping and we're almost done when he adds "Okay, I'm finna get a lil mo' shit lined up for the day and then I'll be home with-chu tonight, we goin' ride out tonight baby girl. Yo' excited?"

"Hell yeah I'm excited as fuck Daddy, yo' know I love to travel with-chu and I can't wait to see some new states and shit. I've gotchu some fly ass gear Daddy and yo' goin' love the surprise I gotchu!" He hates for me to spoil surprises so he tells me that's what's up and before we hang up we both say "I love you." I can't believe I just pulled this shit off. I'm sure Kam is in the driver's seat rolling his eyes as we go from the 'burbs back to our trap territory.

The system bangs hard while Kam is singin'. I'm too busy trapped in a memory of a few years ago. I just turned eighteen and this year Jay had been really laying down the law, using fists instead of words and was gone for more days than not. I was in a dark place. I was too embarrassed to tell Dee the way that he was treating me, hell, I gave Jay my muthafuckin' everything and all he can do is slap me to the floor or throw another fist; He kept accusing me of stealing pills when Lil Trae was steady popping them. My face was full of tears that day and the depression was worse than usual when I got the idea. Hell, why don't I just run away and never fucking come back; who would really miss me? Not Jayceon Michaels! The next few days while Jay was away I used Lil Trae to help me think of an escape plan. Our brother-sister relationship gave him the edge to help me find my way out, but he knew how Jayceon was, well, still is and it's more than obsessive.

The dark night hid my fear when Lil Trae drove me to one of his homie's dope houses, one friend that Jayceon wasn't cool with, and he gave me a few hundred. I didn't even pack anything, just a draw string bag with a few pairs of clothes and left my phone. I can still feel the fear of meeting the Mexican dude they called Chico tatted literally from head to shin. He didn't speak English too good and looked at me like a trade between the two street dudes. Lil Trae took me to a room upstairs and all that was inside was a bare cum-stained mattress, a leaky roof with rain falling inside and the closet was literally boarded shut. The window gave me a view of the shitty city and he asked me if this is what I really wanted. I couldn't even say a word without crying so I just embraced him and shook my head. I told him to not change his number in case I needed to call him. He reassured me that dudes downstairs were some old friends of his and I'd be safe. Roaches, ants and some other bugs kept circling around us in the tiny ass room. I shut the door after Trae left and kept the lights on. I was too scared to go downstairs, too afraid to tell Jay to pick me up because I was attempting to run away from the game and too desperate to let Trae know that I'm more than afraid. I cried on that mattress for hours. A day had passed and I was still groggy from trading Chico fifteen bucks for a Xanax bar when a familiar voice spoke from the wooden floor boards. Was I trippin' off a bad high? It was Killa Kam downstairs. Why the fuck is he here? I got so excited that I ran to the beginning of the staircase, stared down like fifteen stairs and called his name like a maniac bitch into the darkness. He was my knight in shining armor to save me from this hell hole and my confused thoughts. He came upstairs after a few shouts. Chico probably told him my name and that Lil Trae dropped me off. We had more than an embrace. Just to see a familiar face made me feel at home again. Our hug that night turned into Kam taking me inside the deserted room, laying me down, telling me that if I wanted a ride back home it would cost and not from the money that Lil Trae gave me. I kept saying no, just pleading to take me home and Jay can pay him a reward while he'll probably beat my ass...I don't want to have sex but he pushed me onto the bed and took advantage. Luckily, if you want to call it luck in my situation, he had a condom in his pocket and he went to work. It wasn't a lust or caring sex session, he made me go from sucking his dick to hammering away at my super tight pussy, and the dark room hid my tears from that night. He kept telling me that I wanted this dick since day one and that he deserved some good pussy for saving me from Chico and his crew. I finally got a ride home and he never told Jay that I had tried to run away. He just said that he took me out because I was "sick of being in this house by myself." We never told Jay and he never asked, hell I'm not even sure if I told Dee, I've been smokin' too much weed and drinkin' too much liquor to really remember. I'm glad at the hotel, I could finally see that it might have been considered a "rape" but with our chemistry since way back, maybe it was the drugs that had me feelin' uneasy about Killa Kam. I got the chance to play Jay for the day, get some good dick and now I'm ready to be Mrs. Michael's, bitches keep hatin'.

Chapter Ten

Florida, the sunshine state, me and my nigga Jayceon made it! We killed hella weed on the ride down, ducked a few state troopers from 65 South to Nashville, mashed on the gas and got onto 24 South that took us straight to Miami. That's where our new connects spot is posted up at. The transaction went down smooth and our trunk of the Chrysler 300 is iced out with four kilos of coke. Hell that's $100,000 just in blow and more pain pills than an addict could ever dream of. See, I knew that Jayceon had different intentions then going to the Florida Keys just to go to Florida. There is never a vacation; it's all grind no play unless it's that gunplay! The Spanish-style houses are more than luxurious with fountains in the front yards and gates hiding their whips and backyards overlooking the ocean. It's getting to be around seven thirty and thank God the hardest part of this trip is done with. Now, it's time to kick back and lay out on the beach. Before that though, we need some rest. It's been a whirlwind of almost a whole day of straight driving. We've blown through 1,534 miles, three ounces of some good ass 'dro and mixed RedBull with a few Perk 30's to stay awake. We're ready to crash. We've only got one more highway to get on and then Jay will pick out a place for us to stay.

After leaving Miami we jumped on our last highway, U.S. 1, and finally pulled into a few different dope hotels. Jayceon wasn't giving him none of his trap money until it met his high standards. We fell in-love once we found the Hyatt Beach House Resort. Outdoor pools, palm trees and our own balcony made us melt. It would be perfect for our morning 'dro sessions and after great late-night sex we can stare out onto the water, down at the pools and be in paradise. Jayceon gets us booked in for a room; the price was hella high. He paid around five or six hundred per night! While I waited in the lobby waiting for Jayceon to finish the business plans, I kept walking around like I was lost. Broachers on the wall told me that there were so many tourist attractions in walking distance. I grabbed a few that caught my eye to show Jay later and he ordered me to c'mon. He finished business and once we got in the elevator with our bags, it felt all too familiar. Luggage stands beside us and Jayceon has the largest smile that I've seen in months. "Babe, can you believe we got the suite on the top floor? Huh? Shit, we 'bout to tear dis room up!" Slapping my ass he pulls me closer as classical music plays and we kiss. Grabbing the Louie Vaton luggage my heels stab the marble tiles on the floor until we get to room 607. Instead of rose petals like the room me and Killa Kam's had, my baby made it rain. Trap money flooded out of his pockets and flew from the ceiling down to the bed and off onto the floor. I felt like we was at a strip club, but instead of five different hos it was just his main bitch, me. "So, whatchu tryin' do now Bae?" Rolling up a whole pack of White Owl's at the light oak dining room table he just shakes his head.

"I don't know Shawtie, it's up to you mama…if yo' wanna just chill we can, make love we can, fuck, yeah we can do that or if you tryin to go stunt on the town…yeah, we can do that too…"

Working on the last blunt he's already lit up one and I'm waiting for my turn when I suggest "Ay, babe, why don't we do this…" I tell him that we should shower up and get fresh, fuck, smoke some good 'dro again and go out to eat.

He nods as Jeezy plays in the background when he just says "sounds good ma." We hit the luxurious shower decked out in mosaic tiles and our favorite granite countertops. Steamy water and foreplay takes us from the bathroom over to the bed when Jayceon starts kissing me everywhere, including my fruit cups. Just like usual he went from kissing and licking on my fruit cups down to my already wet kat and he ate the pussy. We flipped it over to the couch by the dining room table and Jayceon hit it from the back, having me face towards the sliding glass door with the ocean staring back. I busted twice, well three times if you count the tasting session and he finally busted all in my guts. Laying in bed together, he keeps staring deep in my eyes as he plays with my hair.

"Baby whatchu thinkin? Yo' lookin' at me all deep like how yo' used to when we first got together! Was it that good Daddy?" I make a cute face with my lips poking out and my eyes all narrow like I'm questioning him seriously.

"Chantell, sex with you is always good, yo' ass neva disappoint, and cha know ah nigga love it cuz you keep that pussy so fresh and so clean!" He starts talking like Andre 3000 and we laugh.

"So, we goin' out tonight? Cuz I still need to fix dis fuckin' hair of minez, it ain't five star status like me!" He laughs and gets up to put his brand new Ecko shorts I copped him and I get dressed. He greets me in the bathroom with a few dead presidents and some butterfly kisses while he just stands behind me watching me put my mascara on. Next is my eye shadow, a rich silver that makes my eyes really pop and I put some hoops in to match my gear. The blunt smoke swirls as Jay drives me over to the hairdresser where I get his favorite look, the one that takes him back to the days when I was at my Aunties. I don't wear this look too much because I hate being compared to the past, but it's a special few days for us. Two hours at Magic's Hair Salon and a twenty dollar tip has me coming over to the Chrysler 300 fly as fuck. Tight twisty cornrows on the top and I kept it tightly curled from the back of my head all the way to my lower back, she flat ironed my side angle bangs to the left. The curled hair she threw up in a clip so it sways just like my hips painted in my favorite pair of Dior jeans.

I get back in the whip with Jayceon and he turns down Games "Special To Me" and says "Damn, Chantell, look at chu baby girl lookin' sexy as fuck for her mayne!" I just smile and we speed over to restaurant row with all the upscale ocean front restaurants and boutiques.

Chapter Eleven

Marriage, no one in the hood does that. I'm already married to the hustle and my paper while I cheat on all that with my main bitch Chantell. Don't nobody get it made official, you just know which couple or pimp and ho is together and on that same shit, and with the pimps they got way too many chicks to pick just one! They do got they main bitch, but even her, a nigga wouldn't marry because there's no need. She does her part as wifey and he'll do his. Why does their have to be some bullshit government piece of paper? This is what I've been thinking about since I left Chi-town, just thinking about what if me and Chantell, what if we would get married? What would it change? She'd still do her same routine I'm sure, well, shit she better and life will still go on. Only difference is that she won't have a ring on the traditional finger, does she remember all rings I've got her from keeping my weight up in these streets? If I told my main crew back home I was thinkin' about making her wifey, they would all laugh dey asses off. I could hear Killa Kam saying "bro's before hos...and... why marry when you already got her on that wifey shit anyways? Just buy that spoiled bitch a new ring and call it ah day playa!"

Lil Trae would probably say "Once you wife her you can't deny her..." He's said that shit to me before but what the hell does he mean? I can deny her anything I want, just like how I can give lil' mama anything I want. For months now I've been scoping out other chicks and their looks don't match up to my five star. Their hair isn't as nice and their jeans don't fit like Chantell's do. All these other hood rat females after my cheese. Chantell is just happy with whatever Daddy give her, except for our current crib, she was pissed about that. I kept tellin' her crazy ass it was temporary but really I knew we'd stay for a few years there. I needed a spot right in the hood to make sure my paper stayed right, my trap houses were okay, and a place that the fiends didn't look out of place at. Could you imagine what thirty fiends at a house party would look like in the 'burbs? That shit wouldn't be good. So, we had to stay in the hood. Even when I fuck some new chick I can't get my main one outta my head. A lot of the time I still think that it's Chantell against the headboard, but then I snap back into reality from that kush high and realize I don't even remember this bitch's name.

I guess I need Chantell, which takes my back to my real question, should a nigga walk down that isle and say "I do?" I've been busy thinking about this before this trip to Florida, before I found out about the miscarriage and even before I cheated on Chantell a few months back. I bought her a gift and I've been waiting for just the right time. We pull up into the restaurant and Shawtie is just in the passenger's seat being quiet with all the site seeing. The system bangs and we blaze half of a fresh J to keep the appetite in play while we joke around what to get.

"Yo' should get some kind of exotic fish, and I'm not talkin' bout my…" she looks in her lap and huge smoke rings flow from her mouth. We both just sit there and fucking laugh. An old wrinkled lady and her dude just walk past us all upty and brisk. Fuck dem. Baby girl steps out like a star and we stunt inside Little Palm Island Restaurant. Chantell gives me a superstar smile as we follow the hostess and at that moment, the pure look of sexy, confident, excited Chantell made me realize that I'm making the right move. She truly is my main bitch, first true love and hopefully she'll say "yes" to be my wifey!

Our Key West shrimp appetizer came first right after our drinks. Chantell ordered a sweet tea, so did I. I'm surprised she didn't get a real drink like one of those fancy girlie drinks…but maybe there's something she's not telling me… "Jayceon Michaels, how did yo' hustlin' ass pick such ah nice place to take me to for dinner tonight?"

A glowing smile stays on her face when I just shake my head "I don't know, I think the plug told me…" We both just smile and laugh, hell there's more money in illegal shit inside the whip than what the whips worth. She starts to take me down memory lane as the waitress refreshes our drinks and gives us more bread in the basket.

"Ay, Jay, do yo' 'member when yo' first told me that yo' loved me?"

A million times that I've said "I love you" pop into my head, which one was the first time? "Yeah, we we're over at cha' boys house over on Warren and we was steady stayin' on that lil roof top spot. We had already drank way too much Beam or was it Jack when I toldchu how I really felt, and I was scared that you wouldn't say it back…" Oh, that was the first time…yeah, that's right. Hell I don't even 'member my brain is so gone from all the stacks I've counted, presidential blunts we've blown and shots of liquor over the years. "Mmhmm…yeah I remember that and I said it back, and den we had ah quickie in that niggas momma bed!" She laughed and just shook her head. "We've had some hella good times babe, mayne, we've really been through some shit dese last five years."

"Yo' 'member that face Dee used to make when I'd pull up to swoop yo' up for ah date at tha movies or off to ah party." I scrunched my face up to match a younger Dee's face, all twisted up like my 'dro and shit. Chantell just clowns as we get stares from the other tables. I ask Chantell if she remembers how mad she was when we moved into our current apartment.

She yells back, like we're in the trap house "Hell yeah I fucking remember! Ohh, I was so pissed because I toldchu we should agree on where we live, but yo' kept claimin' we had to set up the tra-"

I cut her off before she puts our shit on blast. "C'mon ma, we in ah fancy ass place not back on South Lafayette Ave!"

The waitress hesitates to come over to our table but sucks it up the fact that she has to serve our ghetto asses and asks us what we'd like for dinner. Chantell places her order of a Sirloin Steak and I get the same. The waitress takes our menus and says our dinner will be ready soon. Chantell's ghetto ass purrs back "it betta be, tuhh!" We both start laughing when she excuses herself to the bathroom.

She invited me with her but I said, "Not in here, this place will care and actually kick you out." She sashays past the bar decked out in its upscale beach feeling, there is French and Latin touches to the décor to match the menu, that's half of what their lighted sign out front boasts. While Chantell takes care of her business all I can do is play with the box in my pocket. Inside is an eight karat diamond ring, but not just white diamonds, it's got both of our favorite colors. I can't wait to see the expression on my wifey's face. I just pray to God that I'm making the right choice. She wouldn't fuck me over and take all the trap money, nah, Shawtie's too caught up in the head games and the love we make.

Dinner wasn't worth one hundred and twenty dollars but the look on her face when I got on one knee was. I grabbed the box from Zales and looked straight in her eyes before I opened it.

"Chantell Saunders, we've already been through hell and back and now we're on our way to the top. I need more than a girlfriend or ah main bitch, so I was wantin' to know if you would want to be my wifey and change yo' last name to mine. Will you be *my* Chantell Michaels?" Opening the all black box the blue diamonds shine to make the outline of a heart with the white diamonds fill in the middle. A set of pink diamonds in the middle carve out the letters "CMJ" to signify "C" for Chantell, "M" for Michaels the last name that puts us together and the "J" for my name.

She gasps so loud that the surrounding tables stare and some silverware drops on the china plates. Tears flow down and mix with our kiss when she says "Yes, Jayceon, baby I will be your wifey, foreva and always babe!" She tells me that she's been waiting for this since day one and I know that right now, them niggas back home might laugh and clown, but Shawtie is my ride-or-die and she's here to stay, believe that! We head back to the hotel and it goes down with kush in rotation, head and 69 and making her call me Daddy. We go a few rounds until she falls asleep naked on my chest with her arm protecting me, protecting us, protecting our relationship and already being a good wifey.

Now I've gotta make her baby's mom when the times right. One day, we'll have a few cute lil' Chantell's and hopefully one Jayceon runnin' round, and it may be at a new place. Maybe babe was right thinking about moving out the hood and to the 'burbs. I fell asleep dreaming of baybay's and a new place 'round the rich white folks.

Chapter Twelve

Kissing me good morning on the side of my cheek I purr back at Jayceon and whisper "Good morning hubby!" Stroking his dick he knows that I'ma fiend for morning sex, even if we went hard last night, but I can tell he's got shit on his mind. Climbing on top I twerk over his thick morning wood and kiss his chest. "I love my new ring Daddy; it looks so fucking perfect!"

He kisses me, deep and more passionate than his love for the trap when he asks me "Do yo' really think we crazy for makin' dis commitment lil mama?"

He's serious so I give him a real answer "Jayceon Muthafuckin' Michaels, who thinks yo' crazy for finally making my dream come true? I've always wanted to be on that wifey status, and soon I'll be on baby mom's status too, shit if yo' worried 'bout cha tricks back home dey can calm tha fu-"

Jay interrupts my stroking technique and walks over to the dining room table. "Shawtie, yo' just gotta realize that where we from no one ever gets married, it ain't neva official. All dey do is stay in and out of ah relationship, like we've been doing…"

What the fuck is Jay's problem? I thought that if you're going to fucking propose, then be for real. Don't be questioning that shit the next morning, this ain't no muthafukin' one night stand ya dig?! Now,

I'm pissed because I feel like a second option, what's his real intentions on making me wifey now...? Did he make me have that miscarriage, ooh, I swear to God why does Jay have to play these fucking games? We'll nigga two can play. I huff and puff my way from the blunt into the shower and don't invite him in either. I sing Mary J's "Be Without You" chorus when Jay pulls the shower curtain back and smiles but I just turn my head and face the wall. "Nigga, fuck you fo' real, I'm sick of how you make me feel" I tell Jay.

Letting the water fall on my body, thinking to myself I say *One day I'm past cloud nine and then the next morning I'm like just a lame ho, nah, nigga neva that.*

Jayceon breaks my thoughts up when he screams "Oh, fo' real Chantell, that's how yo' goin act?" He's serious like Jody in Baby Boy when I just yank the curtain to shut it in his face, again. That'll teach him I tell myself.

Adding "Yeah, nigga it's like dat, tuhh either come get it or get off it...I'm sick of dese dumb ass games yo' ass always tryin' play with ah bitch!" I scream at the beige shower curtain when all of the sudden the door slams. Washing off the rest of my Dove body wash I race out the shower, we both fuel off this drama fighting shit. It's just how we were made, it's been like this since the beginning, it's all me and Jayceon know. His jeans and 4x baggy tee are already on while he starts to put his belt on, next is the heat when I throw my hands in the air. "What tha fuck is yo' doin? Whatchu goin' leave and go fuck some Florida bitch, then comeback and find me on the beach and make it up? Huh?! I swear-" Jayceon gets in my face, closer than I'd like because once he starts this shit there's really no going back. I'm not tryin' to put a hole in this hotel's wall or break another lamp like when we stayed in the Hyatt.

"Chantell, this the childish shit I'm fuckin sick of, all yo' are is ah selfish fucking-"

My reflexes kick in and I slap Jay with the same hand that he put my new ring on. Oh fuck, here we go! His head swivels and swerves back at me like a crazed tiger. Snapping, he slaps my face hard, harder than the usual fights and I fly over to the floor by the ironing board.

Tears just flood down my face. The sting is worse than some honey bees and Jay stands over me.

"Say somethin' else bitch, let me know what's good!" He's on a high from the fight because he yanks me off the floor and slams me on the bed, harder than the night that I lost the baby. Fists and fucking slaps turn into my screams and stinging pain again, it's another round, another fight and another day that makes me wonder if this is how love is supposed to feel. Growling at me he hisses "Tell me you're fuckin' sorry, you fuckin' bitch!"

I usually say what he wants to hear to stop the fight, but with us both gasping for breath I just say "Nigga, fuck you. I hate you, I swear I do, put that on Lil Trae and our traps!" A back hand collides with my already red face and he finishes it with another backhand to the position I started in. His whole body setting on my torso so I can't even move. Spitting up it doesn't hit his face but it infuriates him. He chokes me, tight as hell and I quickly run out of air. I try to move his strong hands and pry his fingers from my throat, scratching and clawing he waits until he's ready to give me air and lets me breathe. I choke on the welcoming breathes as he just mean mugs me.

Sneering back he smiles when he lets me know "If yo' ass hate me so much then gimmie that ring back."

I don't know what to really say, because I know deep down that it's a love-hate relationship and I've worked hard for this ring, hell no I'm not giving it back, I'd rather sell this shit. Housekeeping comes from the door and knocks follow, it reminds us where we're at when he gets off me.

I race into the bathroom because I'm still naked and he tells the maid bitch that we don't need new sheets right now. He tells her to comeback in a few hours when her Mexican accent agrees. The lighter flicks and I get dressed in the bathroom. This isn't how I pictured the next day after we got engaged. This life isn't how I pictured it either after all these years, but that's how the hood is, it keeps you sucked in that cycle all your life until the day you die. That's what Auntie always said to me and Dee growing up, maybe she was right.

"Chantell Michaels, where yo' at babe?"

Fixing my hair I just tell him "hold on!" and finish what I'm doing.

Being so impatient he walks into the bathroom with his shirt off, jeans on and dick in hand. "Yo' tryin' to let me make it up to you?"

Staring at him blankly I say "Why do we fight like that? Is it because yo' addicted to the make-up sex or the fact you like to put yo' fuckin' hands on me?" I tried to cover the hand prints and heat with some foundation and blush, but I could still feel the outline of his fingers. Creeping up on me he tries to kiss me when I jerk away. "Nah, nigga, get the fuck away! Do you see my face? This shit hurts and I'm sick of this being how we show our "love" ya feel me?" He knows how to make me shut up and give in because he carries me to the bed, arms flailing and all when he lays me down and holds my thighs open. Kissing, sucking, licking and finger fucking gets me from saying "stop" to "don't stop" while I pant and say my usual loving making phrases. He finishes me off, I bust a nut and he comes up and French kisses me, our tongues are intertwining. "Yeah, yo' still hate me? Yo' can't say "no" to me cuz I'm Jayceon Michaels, the nigga dat yo' call Daddy and yo' soon-to-be husband…" I just shake my head and he puts it in missionary. We slow grind for a minute and I tell him that no matter what I'm going to love him. He told me that I need to realize that half the time I start these fights and if I would stop giving so much attitude we would be better off. I told him to shut the hell up and stoke faster, he smiled and smashed. We got ready for our day.

Jay decides to drive to a few boutiques and let me cop some new out-of-state gear. Then we headed over to the beach in front of our hotel, my swimsuit looked so crisp white that I could be on my model status when Jayceon's phone goes off. Like usual he answers "What's good?" A look that I haven't seen in years molds into form his face from happiness to pure terror. "Wha-what…When? Who tha fuck killed my nigga? What hospital is my lil brah at? Oh my fucking God, yeah, nigga we on our way!" I stop strutting down the sandy beach and ask Jay what happened. A small voice just mutters out in pure shock and disbelief "Lil Trae got shot!" Racing into the lobby, up the elevator and shooing the house keeping away from our drug infested room we get packed up. Hitting the highway in the 300 I just shake my fucking head in disbelief. Why would God take my brother from me? Who's going to pick me up when Jayceon won't, help talk me through the pain and babysit our kids and someday his godchildren? And, who in their right mind would start beef with Jay? By killing Trae, you've fucked with not only our nigga but the rest of our crew too. Damn, there goes the good news of being engaged. We're on our way to a funeral and autopsy results too.

Chapter Thirteen

*I*t's damn well near nine degrees and we've just touched down in our city. Our first stop is over to Lil Trae's mom's house, Mrs Sammie, to pay our respect and give our condolences. Lil Trae was off and on with his mom. She used to be addicted real bad to heroin. She started using crack towards the end of one addiction but eventually got clean after two or three rehab programs. Once she finally got clean, Lil Trae was grown. He just turned twenty, that's when he would stop over there sometimes and check in on her and catch up. It was hard for him to act like he still wasn't hurt from the words she said or how she kicked him out at twelve, back when we all were kids. I'm sure her selling the food stamps for a rock or stealing his DVD player or gold chain for a hit off the pipe affected him, even to his last days he hardly talked about Mrs Sammie. Back when his mom kicked him out and kept her boyfriend of the week in the house, that's how Trae and Jayceon got so close. Lil Trae became his wingman and right hand man in these streets, from hittin' licks, stealin' whips, chasing the girls and hosting the hottest parties; they did it all together. That's part of the reason why Jayceon lets him crash on our couch or crib any night of the week and gives him free pills and split the Grape White Owls together, they were brothers and if Lil Trae had darker skin you'd believe they were blood brothers.

"Hey Mrs Sammie, how are yo' holdin' up?" Jayceon asks as soon as we start to go up the porches steps. Shaky hands clinging onto a Newport show how devastated she is while she just keeps sobbing.

I ditch Jayceon and give her a warm hug out in this cold ass weather, whispering "Mrs Sammie I'm sooo sorry for your loss mama. We all loved your son, Lil Trae was our lil brah and I promise to you and him we'll find whoeva did this!"

She accepts my promise but still not believing all my words, replies "Thank you hunnie..." I cried and so did Jay, the others who were crowded around Sammie's space heater inside kept replaying their favorite memories of Lil Trae.

I was doing the same thing in my head too, like when he stopped Jay from kicking me in my face in one of the first argument fueled fights we had. Lil Trae also talked him out of shooting me at close range back when we moved into our first apartment, Jayceon and Killa Kam went back in the living room and smoked another kush filled zig-zag while Lil Trae stayed behind and helped me up onto our bare mattress. He told me the same thing then as when I let him in on the news of my miscarriage "Shhh...it'll be okay Shawtie..."

"Chantell..." Sammie and Jay were staring at me. "Who was Lil Trae beefin' with before all dis shit happened?" I tried to put Trae's comforting words in the back of my mind but they were all I could focus on right now. Kids screamed and fought over who was getting the last grilled cheese and who was next on the card game War.

"Shit, I don't know..." I was thinking so hard my head hurt or was this headache from the pain of losing my best friend and not knowing who did it?

"What 'bout that lil white bitch who was tellin' us to stay strapped up?!" I blurt as Jay and Sammie and her man talk about what the days before Lil Trae's death lead up to. Each of them looking at me like I was crazy so I reminded them about the incident. "Yeah, chu know who I'm talkin' bout...her mom OD'd and she was over at Ray-Ray's...she jumped in her piece of shit car and told us all to stay strapped up because her and her people we're feelin' to handle the situation!"

Jayceon shakes his head and Sammie gets held by her man because all she can do is just cry her eyes out. The kids inside stay busy with games to keep from hearing Sammies cries, the sadness that only a mother can feel, which makes me think of the child I could have had. We stayed at Lil Trae's mom's house for almost two hours and decided it was time to leave. Next stop is over to the crib. I feel like we both were dead ass tired and needed to recharge the batteries in our triple beam scales and ourselves. The ride home was quite silent until I told Jayceon "Babe, do you think that white bitch did it? She ain't have enough heart to hold ah gun let alone shoot the strap...right boo?"

Jayceon treats me like a weary child and just agrees "Yeah, Bae, it probably wasn't her..." We pull up to the crib and it's hard to walk up the steps, Trae ain't here to lead the way but at least I have Jayceon.

"What the fuck!" Grabbing the heat from his waist he's on his CSI shit like he just pulled up to a crime scene, scoping shit out. "What is it Jay?" I'm scared because he never pulls the heat out unless he really feels threatened. Stepping inside he tells me to get in the car and have it running.

Jay does a walk through on our apartment and comes back out fifteen minutes later. The wind whips his tee shirt like a white flag. He looks more pissed than when he heard about Lil Trae and a knot in my stomach got twisted and tied. "Somebody broke in our fucking crib!" I just stare at the steps, I feel stunned. Who would be brave enough to rob a Chi-Town legend like Jayceon? A jack-boy, a stick up kid, that crazy white bitch and a pack of haters would, but, what I just realized is "wasn't Lil Trae watching over our house while we left?" Jay said "Yeah, that's right...we had him watch it. I feel like ah fucking killer, if I would have know that my nigga would be dead I would've just kept him off guard or taken him with us." Jayceon starts to break down and we both cry as we speed through the city. We're off to the East Side trap, where Killa Kam better have some truth into what happened in the last forty eight hours.

"Yeah, that's exactly what it looks like my nigga..." Killa Kam and Jayceon we're still trying to get the details together about Lil Trae's murder and our house being broke into. "So, who tha fuck jacked us?"

They passed some good ass 'dro around and play detectives, retracing their steps in the last few days. Killa Kam suggests it was those d-boys from a few blocks away, a whack crew called Sunset Killa's. It's a small group of wanna-be goons who formed their own pack, probably because they got rejected from the more organized gangs. Their motto is they kill somebody before sunset; that's their initiation. Inhaling the 'dro Jayceon shakes his head. "Hell nah it wasn't them pussy ass niggas from Sunset...I think it was someone much closer to Trae, someone who knew his schedule and shit. I really think you or Ray-Ray had ah hand in it, ya'll knew me and Chantell were on vacation and shit."

Killa Kam started to protest when Jayceon says "Oh, by the way congrat's ya'll on the engagement!" A big weary smile crosses my face when Kam congratulates us. Can he still see where Jay smacked me at?

I fall asleep on the couch and when I wake up it was just me and Jayceon. "Babe, where'd everyone go?"

His jaw stayed tight as he mouthed at me "out." I asked where to like a six year old and he got even more pissed. "I got in ah fight with Kam and he left. Will yo' go make me somethin' to eat? I'm hungry as hell!" It doesn't feel weird at all to make ourselves at home in somebody else's house, we did it all the time growing up. I go to the run down kitchen and there isn't shit inside except some off brand mustard, Heinz ketchup and a gallon of milk. It looks glowing from here like it's been sitting so long that it's a light bulb for the fridge.

"Babe, there ain't nothin' here..." He just stands up and leads the way to the whip. We're driving to go pick up some food when I ask him at the fourth red light "Where's all the work from Florida at? Have you distributed it already? When are we going back home to *our* bed and *our* kitchen and *our* food?"

He's already impatient when he answers as we take off from the red light "The work is over at Ray-Ray's. I can't trust a nigga like Kam or Ray-Ray but outta the two of 'em I think Ray-Ray is more reliable. For right now it's my only other choice. The shit won't be there long." Jay keeps informing me "We would've been back in our crib but it's a fucking crime scene, shit, me and Kam went and got all the illegal shit out and checked to see what was missing while yo' was 'sleep." I was waiting for him to tell me what was missing but he pulled into a Rally's. He orders his food and mine, and we share a huge sweet tea. A few burgers and fries later Jay tells me what he saw earlier. "What's missing yo' asked me earlier? My main nigga Lil Trae! Our muthafuckin' stash in the safe! Two guns and whoever did it fucked up the whole crib. Shit is just thrown or broken everywhere!" Tears mixed with straight anger hit both me and Jayceon's face, we're familiar with being the victims of a break-in, that's part of the reason why Jayceon started hitting licks when he first hit the scene. We were supposed to go see where the hell Killa Kam is and I pray to God with all this bullshit with the crib and my brother's death that Kam doesn't decide to tell Jayceon what happened between us. If he does, Jayceon might be losing not only a brother and best friend but he'd lose his wifey too! We passed the trap just to see who was over there and Jayceon decided not to stop, he can't be seen cryin' in front of his people and shit so we make it back to Dee's house. We decided to just post up here for the time being, fuck the apartment for tonight and tomorrow is always a new day. Dee is always a great host for parties we all ended up smokin' on some loud, drinkin' Goose and Jayceon and Dee's mayne Jamal drank shots of Beam. Domino's, Spades and Windows Media Player kept our night going hard until the next morning.

Chapter Fourteen

I woke up before Jayceon and snuck over to Dee's room. I was hoping that she would be up and ready to talk when I tip-toed over to her and Jamal's room. The door was open just enough for me to see Jamal laid out sleeping and I couldn't see Dee so I went downstairs to the kitchen. A warm aroma that smelled like bacon and biscuits led me to Dee in her boy shorts and a wife beater. Greeting me into the kitchen she smiles and says "Ay mama what's up?" I give her a hug around her shoulders as she tends to the food and I grab a seat beside the laptop sitting on the kitchen table. She smiles at me while she finishes singing her Keisha Cole song and tells me "turn dat shit down, I ain't tryin hear her when I got my best friend here wit me dis morning!" We both giggle and start talkin' shit about last night's fun times, trying to sugar coat the pain that's really deep inside us all about Lil Trae's death and the break in.. "Nah, bitch, yo' was tha one tryin' say you could out drink me!" I just rub my face with my hands and keep shakin' my head. "Well if yo' ass wouldn't of one up'd me and shit with dat nasty ass mix you made I woulda won! And yo' know dis mayne!" She is still determined that I'm wrong. "Nah boo, see that's how I figured out chu was ah light weight lil mama!" We both keep denying shit while I light up another cigarette and Dee is in rotation too. It's weird because Jamal and Dee always share cigarettes where we only put that blunt in rotation usually unless we're really low on cigarettes. The bacon gets cooked in the skillet and fried potatoes are next, the biscuits been done their just chillin' in the oven to keep warm. Scrambled eggs are set, I'm ready to eat. I wanted to tell Dee how pissed I was 'bout our crib getting hit and how incredibly sad I am that Lil Trae is gone when Jayceon stumbles down the stairs.

Changing the topic of the house it makes Dee swivel to see who's awake and we both start clownin' on Jayceon. "What's good babe? How'd you sleep?" We all knew that last night was the first time in forever that Jay threw up from drinking and he knows where I'm finna go with this. "Yeah, yeah, you two crazy ass bitches, I admit it, I threw up! After that I was straight, but I'm mad I got some on my Ecko shorts that Shawtie bought me…shit, if you guys really wanna clown did you see that nigga Jamal? His ass threw up way worse than me and started cryin' and shit…" Jay keeps laughin' and looks around for his dread head ass. "Where tha nigga at? Don't tell me he still sleepin' and shit!" That makes Jay laugh even harder as he's looking for a cup to pour some Kool-Aid in it. "Damn Dee where yo' ass keep all tha got damn cups? Can't a nigga get somethin' to drank in this bitch?" We all laugh and I jump up and get my baby something to drink. Jayceon takes my seat and I sit on his lap when I get back with the blue raspberry Kool-Aid.

Before we kiss I ask him "Did chu brush yo' throw up mouth out?"

I could tell he got pissed on callin' him out when he snorts back "Did chu drunk ass brush yo's dis morning?" I tell him no and we laugh. We both start to go to the bathroom when we hear the water running. "Oh, shit, Jamal's up!" we scream at Dee. She just shakes her head and starts singing another Keisha Cole song. Since there's only one bathroom we wait for Jamal and tell him good morning, he just says "what's up" all sleepy and we cram in the bathroom. We brush our teeth and take ah shower together.

"So, Daddy what we goin' get into today?" Jay puts some of Jamal's body wash in his hands and lathers up when he lets me know "We goin' to go find out where that nigga Kam is at and I need to go check on the crib and claim it back as mines. We just gotta clean it up and shit and secure it…" The water pours down on us and I'm worried about Jayceon seeing Killa Kam. Would that nigga really rat me out to Jay about our private hook-up? Not at a time like this. Damn, I wish my lil brah was here to talk to him. I'd give anything to have him hug me and tell me that it would be okay. I rinse off and Jay is getting geared up for the day, we met up around Dee's make shift kitchen table. It's really an outdoor patio table but she don't give ah fuck, and we don't either. Breakfast was great. We all slammed on Dee's buffet and try to laugh some more about last night, hoping the conversation wouldn't get sad. Jamal already has some Beam mixed with his Kool-Aid and Jayceon put some Goose in his cup to ease his pain. Dee and I aren't drinking when she asks me what we're doing today. Stuttering Jay's plans between chews of food she just smiles.

"Yeah, that lil nigga Kam should be around, if not it'd make him look guilty…" We all just stare at her.

Jay says "What?" When Dee explains herself. "Isn't it fuckin' weird that when both ya'll leave, how many states away and shit that not only does one of your main soldiers die but you're house gets robbed too. Was Lil Trae there to watch it while ya'll left? Chantell didn't let me know before you guys left…" I turned red a little because I hope this doesn't bring up anything to do with us spending the night together.

"Yeah Dee Lil Trae was staying there to watch our shit, but here's what gets me. Lil Trae didn't get murked in our crib, there's no blood in the crib and Lil Trae wasn't found in there. Thank God because the work, scales and my safe was in there and we don't need tha muthafuck-in' cops in dere." Stabbing a potato he continues "But, whoever killed Trae probably knew where my shit was at cuz we got robbed, and this nigga right chere is ready to go to war. They killed my lil brah, robbed the crib and I hope dese streets don't think I'm finna let dis slide!"

We all eat silently for a moment. It feels like in remembrance of Trae when Jamal speaks up. "Cha, that's what Dee talkin' bout. She just thinks that it's shifty since ya'll left that Killa Kam was the only main nigga in the crew here besides Trae. Now one of those boys that 'manages' one of yo' traps coulda got jealous too. I'd check in on all dem asses!"

Ray-Ray pops into my head and I can see the wheels turnin' in Jay's head. We've got some suspects and Jayceon is ready to find out the killer like it's one of those James Patterson books. After we eat I offer to help Dee with the dirty plates and pans while Jayceon gets a head start on our day. Kissing me from behind while I'm at the sink he tells me "Daddy goin' go investigate, I'll come getcha in a lil bit so you can kick it wif Dee..." I asked him where he was going to first and he let me know "I'm finna go check on Ray-Ray's crazy ass!"

I get one more kiss when I offer "Why don't I meet chu over at the East Side trap babe? Dee can drop me off then I can leave withcha...is dat cool Daddy?" He nods and my plan is in place, if me and Dee can get to Kam first to confront him on not saying shit to Jay, I will remain safe. If not, well I might up end six feet deep, but let's hope it won't escalade that far if Jayceon gets to him first! "Girl why do yo' want me to drop you off at Kam's before Jayceon? I gotta hair appointment in an hour...hell it takes yo' ass two hours to get ready!" We both laugh when I roll my neck and cluck the roof of my mouth. "Tuhh bitch we gots to get ova dere before Jayceon, so I can live to see anotha muthafuckin' day, ya feel me!" I start to brush my hair and get ready to put it up in my clip when I reveal my plan. "See, Dee, if I don't get there befo' dat nigga then Kam won't hear me tell his ass to not say shit to Jay about our hook-up! It keeps me from being six feet deep and yo' without ah sister!"

She cackles back and just says "uh-huh." I'm finally ready by the time Dee gets behind the steering wheel. We take the back roads to Killa Kam's trap in her '05 Dodge Charger, Jamal is left behind, the bottle still pouring in his cup.

Knocking at the door I'm groaning at the long wait at the East Side trap when Killa Kam finally opens the door to let me and Dee in. "Ay, what's good cha'll? Dee, shit, I ain't seen you in a while, what's that nigga Jamal up to?" They bullshit talk our way in and I didn't see Jay's 300 in the surrounding parking spots, but I'm finna play it safe by looking in the house too. I walk past these two and take a sweep through the living room so I can listen or see if there's a presence of Jayceon. I'm going for it, fuck it, and I announce to Kam "Ay bruh, have you told Jayceon about what we did?"

He takes his glance off of Dee and mugs me. "No. Why would I say shit to him? I wanna stay his partna..." Now we're locking eyes and Kam can see I'm not playing, I don't have time for games and I need an answer. Dee butts in saying "Ya'll better be honest to each other because if Jay finds out it's going to hurt both of ya so no need ta lie to save your ass. Jay would probably kill both of ya and replace ya." Her words were cold and true so we just kept staring back and forth to each other. "Look, I ain't say shit and that's my word. Chantell won't admit it because she know's dat she can easily be replaced! Any hood rat bitch can get makeup, dress up and throw some gold rings on..." Shaking his head he walks into another bedroom.

I keep mouthing to Dee "oh hell nah" and shake my head in disgust. Who does he think he is? I've been with Jayceon for five years. He's only got a year on me for who has known Jay the longest, but that don't mean shit in *my* book. I've been the one with the quarters on the weekends for visits at the prison when he did bids and right beside him counting the profits from the drugs. I've been through it all, unlike Kam who pretended to be down when Jayceon was down and out. I can't take any more of this shit and start telling Killa Kam what it really is!

"Nigga you need to be mo' worried about yo' ass if you lyin'! Tuhh, who tha fuck was here for Jay with quarters on the weekends when he was locked up? Not yo' slut chasing ass. Nope, not at all!" He starts to argue about some scenario, like if I was in the same position I would've chased my mayne than visit a friend locked up. The door swings open and it's Jayceon with a red face and Gucci shades on the top of his head. We both quit talking and turn to face him, has he been standing behind the front door this whole time or did he just pull up?

"Uh, uh, hi baby. What's good?" I don't want to even ask him why he's pissed, let alone stare at him in his eyes. "What the hell was all da screamin' about?" We all just shake our heads like we don't have a clue in the world what Jay's talking about. "Not shit brah, what's good withchu?" Lighting up a cigarette Kam is trying to play coy and I've got to be more confident to cover this shit up.

Dee say's "How's dem profits nigga, you leave for a few days and yo' probably tripled yo' money huh nigga?" She smiles and for that minute

I feel like shit will be okay; no one will get hurt or die. Then we can go on ahead and see who hurt our lil brah and go cop some airbrushed shirts.

Jay just shakes his head and says "What we're you guys just talkin' bout? I heard my damn name and somebody betta keep it real! Why ya'll referring to me bein' locked up? Yo' got under covers sellin' to me nigga?! My main partna' already dead and gone, we still ain't solved the real problems, so why the fuck ya'll talkin' shit 'bout me, huh nigga?!" Glancing at Killa Kam's way, ever since Jay heard 'bout Trae he can't trust nobody, so he's even more suspicious of his own crew. Who's going to do him wrong like they did his lil brah?

Killa Kam just mugs and says "Like I said brah, ain't not shit 'bout chu…me and yo' bitch was talkin' bout when Lil Jim got locked up…" Jayceon walks past the big screen T.V. and around the living room coffee table. Jayceon sticks his hand out to give him dap but reaches for his heat with the other hand and pistol whips that dude. Bam. Clack. Thud. That was the sound of Jayceon pistol whipping Killa Kam, the steel hitting him across his face and the thud of when he hit the floor. Fuck. I don't even know if I should try to deny it, calm him down or say I'm sorry, one wrong move and Jayceon could hurt me or kill me. Dee just needs to leave and save herself. I wouldn't forgive myself if Jayceon did something to hurt her. She's not the one who cheated. She's not the one who put up with his abusive ass for all these years. She's not the one who deserves this shit.

Killa Kam is still sprawled across the floor when I rush over to Jayceon. Grabbing my throat he walks me backwards until my back is pinned against the wall. "Tell me the muthafuckin' truth bitch!" His face is redder than when he came in and my air supply is almost cut off before he jerks his hand off from my neck and stands there for an explanation.

Coughing first I finally get the voice I need to let Jayceon know "Yes, Jayceon I wanted to be…cough…like you. I fucked around and cheated on you BEFORE you gave me the ring and before we left town." Coughing is the only sound in the whole house. No fiends are going to play a witness in the murder that I feel Jay is going to commit.

He's stunned. "You, you, fucking cheated! Chantell are you fucking serious?" His voice was deep and filled with question, all I could do was just nod to agree. "I swear ta God, you fucking bitch!" Jay throws his hands in the air, rushing down his face and hauls off and slaps the shit out of me. I stumble back and crumble to the floor. Crying and sobbing are background noises to Jayceon making me get back up by my hair. Dee is just standing in the middle of all this and not saying shit, Kam is still on the floor. Jay takes me to the car and Dee races outside to the porch, Kam tries to stumble out, trying to walk off the pain and play it off. The whole way home was filled with Jay's cussing, no music, no laughter just a pissed off Jayceon. Cussing at cars, icy roads, cold wind and the fact that I sucked another nigga's dick. We hit another red light and he just keeps repeating "my down-ass bitch, fuckin' some other dude from the crew, what the fuck!" I keep my hands to myself, the aggravation of how many times Jayceon cheated on me had me swallowing the hos phone calls, and I am trying to keep my anger down before we end up on the news. Pulling up to a Target I asked Jayceon curiously "Why is we stoppin' here Jay?" Putting the car in park by a light post he just says "Didn't you want an EPT test, we have been doing a lot of fucking lately, and I know you wanted to get pregnant..." I instantly get happy, forget all the fowl shit I was thinking and chirp "Yeah babe, I almost forgot, I've been so busy lately with hurrying back to Chi-town and-" He sneers in my face, taking the joy away when he adds "yeah, you have been busy you cheatin' ass bitch!"

My hopes of being pregnant soar down because if I am, all I will have to hear for nine months is the same thing that bitches on Maury hear every day. "I'm not tha baby's dad, bitch I need ah DNA test!" Jay runs in and grabs the test, a twelve pack of beer and a new box of condoms, ouch, that was a slap in the face. We never use rubbers, now he's just being an ass, to rub in the fact that he thinks I'm dirty as if I'm not his fully. I light up a Marlboro while he throws the bags into the back, damn, where to now? Next stop ends up being the crib to clean up the damage. We're on our way. Earlier I told Dee to text me when she gets home safe and let me know how Kam's head was. She promised she would and I told her if I didn't answer I'm dealing with Jayceon's wrath. She lol'd on the text back to me but knew I wasn't playing. Getting her text before we made it home got my mind off shit, I told her what Jay bought from Target and before we could get too deep in a talk Jayceon pulls up to the house.

"What's tha stick say?" Jayceon walks into our tiny bathroom with a beer in hand and I'm shaking. "+, that mean's its positive, oh my God, baby I'm pregnant!"

I start to hug Jay and his face is stale, cold, and he just rolls his eyes and slurs "shit, why should I be excited, what if it's another nigga's baby?! Huh?" That was the blow that hurt, like when he pistol whipped Killa Kam, did Jayceon really just regret me and my baby news like that? I force him out the bathroom and slam the door. What am I going to do? All I've ever wanted was to be Jayceon's wifey and baby's mom. A child would complete us and slow his hustle, but not if this baby isn't his. I would lose everything that I've loved for so long. That would hurt more than when my mom OD'd when I was nine. It would hurt more than moving in with my Auntie and becoming the unwanted child or being looked at like another SSI check. It would hurt more than all of the slaps, violent arguments and hurtful words between me and Jayceon. My life would be turned upside down like our headquarters above the corner store. I just sit on the bathroom floor and let the bugs crawl over me, roaches and all. I was more than depressed and Jayceon wouldn't even come in and try to apologize for earlier. It must have been a few hours later, the living room is completely cleaned up like nothing happened and Jayceon is asleep on the couch. T.V. blaring MTV while the light in the kitchen is bold and inviting me over. I call my sister and best friend to ask her what in the hell I should do, I want to save my boo, my engagement to one of Chi-Town's greatest and keep our family together.

"Did you take the test Chantell?" Dee was quiet, not her usually boisterous self.

"Yeah, it came back with a plus sign, I'm really pregnant…"

She screams with excitement when Dee tells me "Oh my God, congratulations baby girl, this is the perfect fix for today's fight! Ya'll goin' to be good parents boo-boo and I'm finna be ah good godparent, me and Jamal's crazy ass!" I hate to get her hopes up but the pain in these next few sentences made her realize that everything's not okay.

"Uh, I'm not excited now. Jayceon didn't even care. All he said was that we'll see who the real baby's dad is and isn't even being supportive. He feels like I was more than unfaithful and is even sleeping on the couch. I just sat in the bathroom for hours to get my thoughts together. He didn't even check on me, call my name to see if I was crying or even bring me somethin' to drink…Dee, what the fuck am I going to do to get him to see that I'm still *his* wifey and main bitch?"

She comes up with the greatest idea, I'm pissed that I didn't think of it when she lets me know "Get an ultra sound. Go to the OBGYN, Planned Parenthood or the Hospital and they can probably tell you the date that the baby was conceived. Take Jay and prove to him that this baby is ya'lls blessing from God and prove that you've always been *his*, and his *faithfully*. That nigga shouldn't count the one night stand that you cheated. Shit, have we tallied up how many times that dude has creeped 'round Chi-Town and out of stateer's?!" I talk to Dee through-out the rest of the morning about future plans and names for the baby. It's almost nine thirty and I haven't slept all night. Jayceon wakes up and stumbles out into the kitchen, four or five beer bottles are carried out to the sink. "A'ight sis, I'm finna letchu go and I will letchu know how tha day goes. I'll keep you posted mama and tell Jamal we said what's up too. Yup, I'm callin' one of dem right now!"

Burping and scratching his boxers he says "Who tha fuck was dat?"

I just stare down at my phone and answer "Dee, nigga who yo' think?" He tells me I don't need to get smart and that he's not going nowhere. "Fo' real if I plan to find out this crucial news yo' ass really ain't goin to go?! How you goin' believe me if yo' don't hear it fo' yo' self? Huh? If me and Dee went you'd say we were lying and probably tell me you'll see me in ten months, long enough to have the baby and see whose it is…"

"No, Chantell, I still feel faded from last night, a'ight?"

"What the fuck ever Jayceon Michaels, you's ah bitch ass nigga fo' dat…dat's cool."

Scooping my face into his hand he points my chin up to his eyes and just holds my face there, jaw clinched tight as he tells me "I still fuck withchu so don't act like I've leftcha. Don't ya ring finger stay iced out still? Is you still wearin' the same gear I boughtcha? Have I took the keys and yo' Coach Purses back? Nah, I ain't done none uh that… let me take a shower and smoke another fat L and we can go to the Hospital. You need to calm the fuck down wit' cha' shit, fo real, cuz babe I will always love you!" Kisses swirl down and Jay shows me for the first time in almost two day's that he still does care. He still does got love for his Shawtie.

"I love you Bae, you know this…" He tells me he does and if I'm wanting some of that morning dick I'd betta meet him in the bathroom immediately. We do our usual morning sex routine and he doesn't even use the condoms he bought yesterday. My baby still does love me.

"Yeah, how'd Daddy's dick do? Huh?" I just have this spaced out cheesy smile as we each light up. "That round was some of the best sex of my life Jayceon, almost as good as back in the day Daddy!"

"Oh yeah?" Jay takes one more puff of the joint and puts it out in the ashtray. Before I can ask why he didn't give me my turn he kisses me with a shotgun and moves me back to the bed, laying me back with more French kisses and caressing hands. "Mmhmm, round two baby? I see yo' on you're A-Game!" Going straight down for another taste of this good-good he slurps and sucks while I grip the sheets and rub his face all in it, he comes back up and I taste the love made from him starting with my fruit cups and finishing down south. Damn, ah nigga has me sprung.

Jayceon drives me over to the same ER that Lil Trae took me to, and this time he parks the car up close and we walk in together. I better not get the same nurse that tried to change me and my life last time, because, a bitch might get punched in her shit for talkin' all that shit. She doesn't know *who* my baby is and where we're at in our relationship. Fuck her and all the others who hate or try and talk they shit. I'm just here to see if we can figure out when this baby was made. I pray that it was with the one that I love with all my heart and not just

98

a booty call. Other girls are sitting there and most of them already have babies or toddlers with them, but I don't see a man sitting beside them. I hope that's not me in the next few years. Jay will always be here for me. We're just going through a rough spot I tell myself while we wait. A nurse with hot pink scrubs on and a short pixie haircut calls my name off her clipboard. Jayceon helps me up and takes me away from my thoughts. We hold hands to the examination room. My feet go up in stir-ups and the jelly is slathered on across my belly. All three of us, Jayceon, the doctor and me all see the black and white ultra sound of a baby, a tiny person inside of me and the doctor lets us know that I'm three almost four months pregnant! I should've known since my period hasn't came in a while, but with Lil Trae gone, the engagement and the excitement of the streets, who Jay can and can't trust mixed with these fiends has me caught up in it all.

"Congratulations Mrs. Saunders and Mr. Michaels!" I correct him as Jayceon caresses my hand. "Yeah, it's Mrs. Michaels, we just got engaged in Florida!" I show off my new ring and he "oohs" and "awws" at my iced out finger. "You're a lucky woman Mrs. Michaels. We'll get you a copy of the ultra sound and give you some pamphlets about the months to come." He wipes me off and leaves. I get my pants buttoned up and Jay gives me such a loving kiss.

"I can't believe we've gotta baby on the way lil' mama!"

I just purr back to him "I know, you're going to be such ah good daddy baby! We'll both make good parents. I can't wait to start thinkin' of names!" He keeps screaming with excitement that if it's a boy it will be named half after him and half after Lil Trae when the doctor knocks on the oak door and steps inside.

"Here's the reading material, ultra sound pictures and some important info." He lets me know that the baby was conceived on September 19th and confirms that Jayceon would most likely be the father, the one night stand didn't get in the way of what me and Jayceon had and still have, now. The doctor also asked us about our relationship, because he was curious about the bruise across my face and how my eye was swole.

"Oh, it's nothing. I fell the other day when I was trying to carry a basket of laundry down the steps. I missed the second one on the way down and fell." How many times has a doctor heard that line I thought, but it's the only excuse that sounded remotely believable. He didn't need to know me and Jay's drama, that's between us and what I share with Dee. Extending his hand he shakes my baby's dad's hand first then mine and we leave out of the hospital holding hands. I've got great news and life is wonderful for the most part.

We go out to breakfast together and celebrate the last few months of freedom before we have a child that connects us. Bob Evans was packed. We should have figured this because it was Sunday. A booth for two and the Pot Roast Melt for me, Jayceon gets a skillet platter with eggs and potatoes. Sipping his sweet tea I keep gushing about how excited I am to have a new chance at becoming a parent with the love of my life. "Baby, I'm so happy to have you as my baby, best friend, fiancé and baby's dad. I can't wait to find out what we have…what do you want? A boy or a lil girl?"

Jayceon scopes out the place while we talk and decides he would of course like a boy, but either one would be a blessing. "If we have a girl, she better understand that when she gets older her Daddy has to protect her from dese squares, lames and dem players! Ya feel me?!" I just keep nodding my head and agree "ain't no lame nigga goin' date our baby girl if we have one. And if we have a son, he's gotta be like his Daddy and get a real down-ass bitch, huh!" We laugh and keep talking about what qualities we hope our child will have, some silly and some fo 'real.

Our food comes and Dee calls. "Ay, lemmie call yo' ass back, yeah, I'm fine. We're out to eat…yeah, I promise I'm finna call yo' back boo!" I couldn't wait to tell Dee but at the same time I really wanted to enjoy the outing with Jay, just the two of us while we're both in a great mood. What a rare time. We both try samples of each other's and decide who got the better plate. I have a good idea and share it with Jay while the waitress re-fills our glasses.

"Babe, what if we take a parenting class or two together?! That'd be awesome and we could learn every step of the way. We need to go buy some baby books and shit too, and I need to go get a car seat and lil Jordan shoe's for the baby." I kept going on and Jay slowed my roll.

"Before we cop new gear for the baby, we need to find out if it's a boy or girl officially, Plus Shawtie, we don't need a damn book or class to raise a kid, our parents didn't need a class." As soon as Jayceon said it I could tell he regretted it. "Well, you know what I mean, babe, we'll be great parents and you know dis…" I just agree and go along with Jayceon's ideas, but I also know that he's going to some classes. He needs to realize what parenting really is all about besides just babysitting. We finish up our meals and Jayceon pays. He gives the waitress a twenty dollar tip and we're off to the trap house, our house.

I turn down the music and deny the blunt in rotation. "Babe, I can't smoke…remember? Ay, but I wanted to letchu know Daddy that we need to consider moving…you promised we wouldn't stay in this dumb ass apartment this long!" Dee is blowing my phone up and I put it on vibrate. I can tell that Jay is thinking as he switches lanes, instead of going home we're onto a new adventure. "Where we goin' Jay? The exit for the crib was back dere."

He tells me "Yeah, I know babe. We're going to a guy who owe's me a favor. You'll see…"

I insist, "We better not be on no run for tha pills cuz I don't wanna get caught and be pregnant and locked up babe!" I tried to sound like I was joking but that reality really did scare me.

"We're not making no runs or anything, just kick back, call Dee or turn the music up." Mashing the gas he informs me "Chantell, I promise on everything I love and on all this trap house money that I'm ready to make you a commitment. You're going to be my wifey, baby's mom and I'm going to move us out the hood. We need to slow our role on that hustle and we'll eventually find out who did Lil Trae in. Life can't go nowhere but up to the top and I'm takin' minez with me!" Did I just hear this dude right? Is he making all of my life's goals a reality? Wifey, check. Baby's mom's status, check. Movin' out tha hood, check. Finding closure for our brother, check and having Jayceon take more caution in the streets, check muthafuckin' mate! Bitches, keep hatin' cuz we're here to stay ahead in this game.

Chapter Fifteen

*J*ayceon hasn't been home in a few days, I've had Dee by my side the whole time. She cooks us some hamburger helper and we've been talking all day about baby names. "What if it's a boy? Yo' goin name him right after his Daddy, another Jr. runnin' around in this hell hole that we call Earth?"

I finish my sip of Kool-Aid she just made and say "Nah, probably not. If it's a boy we'll probably name him Jayceon Trae Michaels, after Jay and Lil Trae you know…" My cup was still full but I just stared in it like it was empty and there was no more left.

"Awwh, that's so sweet Chantell! That would mean a lot to both of dem! What if it's a girl, ya'll got a name for that yet?"

I shake my head and tell her "Nope, we don't have a girl name…I still need help with choosing one, I wanted to get one of those baby books but Jay refuses to buy one." We both laugh and Dee hands me a huge paper plate of food. Comedy Central is our background noise as we both eat, watch T.V. at times and talk about the past and future. "How long you been with Jamal now, what eight years, ya'll goin' to be like me and Jay and tie da knot?"

She swallows hard "Hell nah we ain't getting married! That nigga already sponge off me as it is, give his ass ah ring and he'd divorce me just to get half of nothin' that I got!" We both clown and giggle. "Girl we already got kids together, ah house and all he needs is a real day job, besides that we goin' be okay. We're not ah young couple like you two." I've been curious if Dee would even laugh if I told her my idea of parenting classes, I didn't want to honestly hear about her and Jamal. I wanted it to be about me and Jayceon.

"What do you think of those parenting classes?" She takes our plates to the kitchen and throws them away. The trash can lid slams down as she says "What about them?"

"Do they really help or is it all bullshit? Did you ever go to any when you were pregnant?"

"Hell nah me and Jamal didn't go to classes, we just had her and learned as we went along…there's times you'll flip yo' shit, lose your temper, fight over snack time and whoop they ass…but I don't think you need classes to learn about that." Damn, maybe Jay is right, just like he usually is. "But, if I had to do all over, I think I would of went to some shit like that. It would be fun to go with you're boo and learn about what your body is going through and how to handle labor a little better. You guys should go!"

"Yeah, but Jay feels like it's a waste of time, like how you said you just learn as you go. That's the type of shit he's on…"

"Well, if you really wanna go, I know that I'm not baby's dad, but I will go with you if you need. Promise." We cross fingers and this is why I love Dee; she's always there for me. We put on a movie and I fall asleep. The last thing I could hear was Dee cleaning the hamburger helper pan and wiping down the stove. The beat down door opens and Jay starts to come in loud as Dee tells him to calm his black ass down. Can't he see I'm asleep on the couch? I pretend to sleep as Dee helps nudge Jayceon my way. "Jayceon Michaels, I heard ya'll are expecting?" A smile glows from his face as he hides the work in the next room, coming out gleaming like the summer's sun.

"Yeah, we sure are. I can't be more excited to start a new place in our lives…why yo' think I'm on my grind to really stack dis paper up? I've gotta move lil mama out the hood like I said I would, then I've gotta calm down on the hustlin' to grow old for my wifey and baby."

They keep talking when Dee asks "Yo' are going to parenting class with lil mama right?" He tries to dodge her question by focusing in on the movie but Dee don't play that shit. She asked him again, this time a little more annoyed.

"Uhm, yeah, I probably will..."

"Whatcha mean probably will? Either you are or you aren't nigga; there ain't no in-between! Tuhh!" She did the eye and neck roll while I act like I'm just waking up, stretching and shit. Opening my eyes slowly I observe who's in the room and say "hi" to Jayceon.

"What's good lil mama? How's wifey doing? What 'bout baby, is it makin' you sleepy?" I tell him that I'm fine, I'm just being lazy and getting special treatment from Dee, my big sis. He offers to go snuggle with me in our room and I look at Dee. She's giving me the vibe that she doesn't care so I take him up on his offer. "Yeah, Daddy, you goin' put me to bed and tuck me in?" I smile and start to sing J. Holiday's song to let him know I'm ready to have some good ass sex and then cuddle while we fall asleep together.

"Mmhmm" Jay says and we're off to the bedroom. I get on top and Jayceon lets me kiss from his chest to the tip when I stare back up and ask "Babe, yo' feelin' to go to class wit me soon?"

He gets a handful of my hair and asks "what class Shawtie? That parenting class?" Nodding while I kiss and lick down there he just says "Yeah, fine, I'll go..." We smash from the back and fast stroke from the front, I try not to be loud since Dee is downstairs or in the next room. We finish and I swallow it. After that I cuddle up in the blankets. I'm too tired to go brush my teeth or throw on some sweat pants or Vickie C's panties. We fall asleep buck ass naked, Jayceon beside me, rubbing my body and curled up tight around me in the covers. It's times like this that I absolutely love, no matter the fights and screaming. Its nights like this that really soothe my soul. These nights keep me going and give me hope that everything will be alright in life.

The sun has stayed up, shining in through the broken blinds and I roll over to face him but his back is staring back. I rub his shoulders and kiss his neck, he finally decides to roll over and face me. Stretching I say "Hi babe, good morning." I snuggle deep into his chest and his arms caress me. "Yo' wanna get ready with me fo' dese classes? It starts at one thirty."

All he can mumble is "what time is it?" with his eyes still closed.

"Uhm…" I roll away from him and stare at the phone sitting on the floor. "Its eleven forty-seven Jayceon…time to get up right?" I wait for an answer but he snores. Getting into the shower I wake up with the smells of vanilla and jasmine, steam swirls onto the mirror. Getting wrapped around a towel I use my finger to write across the mirror "I love Jayceon Michaels <3" underneath it I put "love, always, baby moms and wifey! Chantel <3"

Getting dressed Jayceon gets ready at the last minute and we're off to our local run-down community center. I hope that we make it there on time. The parking lot is not too full but there's probably twenty or twenty five people inside, including our instructor. There's snacks too. I grab a granola bar and Jay grabs us some drinks. The teacher, Miss Maddison, introduces what we'll be learning, how long the classes will last and lets us go around and say a few things about ourselves. Metal fold out chairs tell their stories and Jayceon won't quit mean-mugging everyone. His phone keeps chirping. It's embarrassing because we're not here to sell bricks or pills, we're here for our future together. Before it even gets to our turn he's already outside and now I'm pissed. I was doing this for us, not for just my knowledge. He can't even sit in the gymnasium. It gets to my turn we're almost done with introductions. All eyes are on me when I speak up and say "Hi, my name is Chantell. I'm here because I just found out that we're expecting. Yes, that's my husband outside." I glance towards the doorway hoping he'd here me somehow and walk in. I continue and say "I'm really excited about learning how to be a better parent than what my drug addict mama was. I'm really excited because this is my first one. Thanks for letting us sign up and participate." I direct the last comment to Miss Maddison and she smiles. The girl beside me seems cool. She's got on cute pink and black plaid pajama pants and a baby phat tee shirt, her name is Raquel and she's a redbone. Curly hair spills down her shoulders and past her breasts, she tells everyone that this is her second child and enjoyed Miss Maddison's class and advice from before, so she had to come back. We all clap and the next four people say their shit. Jayceon still ain't back in yet and we move on to the introduction of week one. I start to tune her out because now I'm more than pissed, I'm enraged. What the fuck is Jayceon doing? I excuse myself from our circle of students and walk outside. This nigga betta have ah good excuse for missing the whole first class. He made me look like a single mother when I'm not on that type shit; we are a team. He's sitting on the bench out front smoking a cigarette on the phone with someone. I walk up to him from behind and stab his shoulder with my fingers, face scrunched up, and he just turns around points to his phone and mouths sorry. Sorry, are you serious right now?

"No, get off that fuckin' phone Jay!" He swirls around, cigarette smoke swaying out of his nose and mouth and says to whoever the fucks on the other line, "Hold up brah…"

"What!?" I just stare back and I can feel the tears of frustration already welding up.

"Why are you on the phone? Aren't we supposed to be in this class together? Yo' dumb ass made me look stupid as hell in there, all by my-self. I'm not a single mom! I have you and all yo' can do is talk to one of yo' nigga's out cha'?!"

"Lemmie call yo' back brah, baby mom's trippin'. A'ight, I'm finna call you in a lil bit brah. Word."

Standing up he just mugs me and asks "What is yo' fuckin' problem Chantell? I was on a business call and you know I'm on the hustle even harder since we've got a little one on the way. I'm tryin' to pull strings so we can stack paper and move you out the hood, that's whatchu want right?! Cuz I'm fine where we're at now. I'm doing this for you and the baby…"

"Yes baby I want to leave the hood and move somewhere nicer but right now yo' main focus should be in here with me listening to Miss Maddison talking and holding my hand. Is this how it's going to be erry muthafuckin' time we come here, cuz if that's the case I don't need-"

"You don't need what? Me here?"

"No Jayceon Michaels, I don't need you out here on the hustle for this hour and ah half…I just need *you* babe. C'mon back in here with me Daddy den once we leave you can go run the streets, c'mon..." I kept giving him my pout face and he slipped the phone back in his Girbaud jeans and grabbed my hand.

"C'mon lets get in here I guess..." We return back to class and everyone has a few flyers in their hand, pamphlets and the schedule for the next nine months. I get my handouts and class is over. As soon as it's dismissed everyone gets up and goes on their way. Jayceon heads out to the parking lot and I make my way to the door when the girl beside me, Raquel, stops me.

"Hey, I just wanted to say hello. I'm Raquel, if you need anything or have questions about class, I've done this before so if you and him need anything, let me know..." We both stop and start to talk.

"Yeah, thanks Raquel, that's really nice! I'll probably be here for each class, and I hope that Jayceon will too...does your baby's dad come with you at all?"

I could tell I hit a nerve when she said "Fuck dese nigga's outcha...I know that sounds messed up but my first baby's dad bounced out right after I told him, called me ah ho and packed his shit up. The dude that got me pregnant this time acts like he goin' stay but his lazy ass won't even get up to come to class or even take me around his family and shit. I look for him to leave once I blow up like a watermelon!" She laughs and so do I, but we both know there's pain behind that laugh and tough facade. We exchange phone numbers and I can tell that even if Jay don't come to class I'll still have somebody here for me, Raquel, and I just hope that she's not the only support I'll have. Jayceon better get his shit together.

We hop in the whip. He's been standing in the parking lot right beside the 300 and looks impatient. "Why are you in such ah hurry to leave?" He gets inside and after I slam the door he tells me "I've gotta make some rounds at the traps today, re-up, and collect numbers. I don't wantchu bein' out chere pregnant and dealing with this hustling shit. So I'm goin' do your job you can just kick back and chill." We head over to Dee's and he drops me off and kisses my forehead. He doesn't even watch me walk up to Dee's front door before he peels off. Jamal answers the door and I find Dee watching T.V. when I break down. I tell her everything that's happened lately, including how I felt abandoned today, and she just lets me cry while we hug in-between me cussing Jay out.

"Lemmie fix yo' somethin' to eat mama...whatcha want? We got sandwiches on deck, eggs with cheese or I can fix some bar-b-que chicken and mac and cheese...What sounds good Shawtie?" Jamal speaks up and votes for the chicken combo when Dee yells at him "Didn't nobody ask yo' fat ass whatcha want...I have company over, so Chantell gets to pick!" I go along with the bar-b-que chicken and off brand mac and cheese. Dee stays in the kitchen cooking up our lunch and all I can do is rub my belly, talking to my baby inside my head. "I will always be here for you, no matter what baby!" It's times like this I wish Lil Trae could come back and put Jayceon in place, help him realize what he's doing and give me a much needed hug. Next week, in a few days on Wednesday is his showing and burial. Too much shit has happened in these past few weeks. After Dee fixes me a large plate I smash and fall asleep on the couch. Dee turns the T.V. down and Jamal goes a few houses down to go try his luck at the dice game. I woke up and it was three thirty, Dee must have just lit another cigarette because the smoke quickly fills the small space. I wave it away and start to sit up on the couch. "Did I tell you about the chick that I met today in class, sis?" She says no and asks me who it was. "Do you know her from the streets or the trap? Cuz yo' don't need to be fuckin' around with someone like that now that you have a baby-" I shake my head from side to side and say "Hell nah boo, her name is Raquel. She already has one kid and this is her second one and second baby's dad. She gave me her number after class and told me that she'll be there for me if Jay doesn't keep going to class. It was just nice to have someone to relate to, someone who knows what I'm going through without explaining all of the late night details...I'm not saying you don't understand Dee, but it was just nice for a new person to be cool about shit, especially when Jay ain't."

"Yeah, I hear ya sister! It is nice to know that someone cares besides the close family members. Have you called her yet? Where she stay at? How old is her other kid? Is her baby's dad around from round one or did he bounce?" I tell Dee that "her first baby dad is gone and I don't remember if she told me how old her first born is now. She didn't say where she lives at or how old she is, we just gave each other our numbers and went our separate ways. Do you think I should call her today or wait til the next class?" Dee asked me when the next class with Miss Maddison was and I told her it was this upcoming Wednesday.

"Shit, call her...let her know that you appreciate the support and ask her questions 'bout herself, make sure she ain't no muthafuckin' lunatic boo." We both laugh and Jayceon's face flashes across my blackberry. "Oh, shit, it's Jay. What that hell does he want?"

"Hello?"

"Ay mama what's good? Yo' busy?"

"Why? I'm sittin' here talkin' to Dee...whatcha need?"

"Meet me out front and hop in the whip, I've gotta surprise for you babe!" I tell him to honk when he's out front and we hang up. Dee asked me what that was all about.

"He said he's got a surprise for me...wonder what it is?" Dee just laughs and says "I hope it's a better time than this morning! If your ass ain't happy Chantell I do want you to know that Jamal and I will make room for you in here, believe dat mama!" I thank her and scoot across the couch to give her another hug. I thank God all the time for putting Dee in my life, yeah my Auntie has helped me but Dee is the only one who remained standing throughout life's ups and downs. This bitch has always had my back since muthafuckin' middle school and she has always made me a part of her life, for the better. I love her for that. She starts to roll up a fresh L when Jayceon honks the horn out front twice, we say our goodbyes and she tells me that if I need anything just call. I told her I will, just like always, if I need her and I bounce out. Jayceon has a bouquet of roses beside the steering wheel and welcomes me inside the whip.

"Here baby mom, I gotchu these and I'm sorry about today..." I smell the roses and they smell so fresh, almost as fresh and delightful as life itself in the good moments.

"What is all this about Daddy? Where we feelin' to go babe?" I set the roses in the back seat and put my Coach bag on the floor board.

He tells me that it's a top secret surprise but we'll be there in forty minutes. I kept asking him if it was lunch or dinner because me and Dee already ate. He just said no and told me its way better than food. We pull up to an all stone building that had "Real Estate" in the sign out front and he lets me know "We bout to go house shoppin' Shawtie!" I squeal with delightment and we walk inside together, holding hands.

"Hi Kathy, this is Chantell and I'm Jayceon." She shakes both of our hands and her office smells like Bath and Body works. "Okay you two, so tell me what kind of house appeals to you?" We both start talking about our needs, concerns and wants. We agree on everything except Jayceon wants four bedrooms. I say we get three, but he's hellbent on four. She get's some listings together and asks if we would like to see a model house and maybe one more for the day since it's getting close to closing time at six. We meet her over to a suburbanite neighborhood called Northbrook, over on the North Side of Illinois. A two car garage greets us and so does Kathy. "Okay guys, this is the heart of a suburbanite area called Northbrook. Typical home value in this neighborhood is around $370,800 and the typical monthly payment is $1,313.00. This home is in the statistic's range, let's go inside." We follow her up the sidewalk that leads us to a stunning red door with matching shutters. Kathy begins her sales pitch as she shuts the door behind us. "Okay guys, this has four bedrooms, three and one half baths, finished basement and all hardwood floors. Sound good already?" Her fake smile leads us into the open floor plan. The kitchen can be seen after the living room invites us inside. A stair case is off to the right. A fancy rod-iron railing tempts us upstairs. We take a tour of the house. The kitchen was decked out with granite counter tops, black appliances and dark mahogany wooden floors. A finished basement included a new GE washer and dryer combo, one of those money saving ones. We go upstairs. I counted seventeen steps before we saw the easy floor plan. A bathroom is the first door on the left. It looks like a hotel bathroom with the fancy showerhead and tiled floor. A spare bedroom lays beside it and on the other wall is a cut out for an office type room. Our master bedroom has a full bathroom and is the last room on the right, right before the baby's room. We discuss a play room and question the concern of having steps and a new baby, but overall we like the house. We can see the backyard from the office window and its lengthy backyard. Green strips of grass shine in the cold winter weather. After another ten or fifteen minutes we're off to one more listing. Before we get in our separate cars the real estate agent asks us how much we think this listing is. Jayceon says 450,000 and I say 380,000. Kathy smiles and says that the listing is in the middle of our guesses. It's actually on the market for 410,000, not counting closing costs and other fees. Our economy and housing market is in terrible shape so she tells us to enjoy these low listing prices. We all smile and we're off to another listing in two neighborhoods away.

"I really do like this area, it does feel way safer."

Jayceon agrees and we take a look at the second house. It's almost identical, except there's carpet, hardwood floors and tile throughout the house. This one has a one car garage, which Jay isn't too happy about and there's a backyard against some woods. That's perfect. We both like that feature. Kathy gives us a higher price than before with this one ringing up at 485,000. We shake hands and she tells us she'll look forward to hearing from us. We tell her thank you and that we'll be in contact. We inform her of the funeral happening tomorrow. "Yeah we'll probably call you next Tuesday or Wednesday because of a funeral." Kathy gives us her condolences and we're back to the trap in no time.

"Whatcha think of dem houses Shawtie? Dey meet yo' high ass standards, huh?" Jayceon laughs and I agree, that yeah, they're more than beautiful. At this moment I feel like life is perfect. My family is finally coming together. The only thing missing is Lil Trae.

"Yo' tryin' spend the night at Dee's again or am I droppin' you off at the crib babe?"

"Where are you 'bout to go?"

Jayceon turns down the music and lets me know "Shawtie, I told-cha I'm on the grind. I've gotta keep hustlin', you know rise and grind til the sun comes up mama. I'ma be safe though, trust that. Yo' mayne ain't getting locked up, not now. Plus, I'm still keepin' an ear to the streets to find out about Lil Trae and why our house got hit…So I'm busy babe." Ugh, this is one of the few parts that I hate about being in love with ah hustler who's married to the game. I just agree and tell him to drop me off at Dee's, fuck the trap above Rick's, I'm don't feel safe staying there by myself anymore. He drops me off and gives me a grand "Here mama, go take you and Dee out on a shopping spree, buy some new shit for the baby and have a good time while I'm in these streets!" We kiss across the console and he speeds off, Dee lets me in and I tell her about the money Jayceon gave me.

"Damn, that nigga keeps you havin' stacks on deck, wonder why?"

I shoot back "Probably because he loves me…and wants to see his Shawtie ball on these hos with fresh gear for me and the baby!"

Dee adds a comment that I hate hearing, especially from her. "Or he feels guilty for staying out in the streets all night, trying to buy you back and keep you from leaving. He's probably fuckin' some of those bitches who live in dem traps too…" I sit at the patio table and watch Dee work around the kitchen fixing her and Jamal some dinner. Me and their two kids Ja'mari and their daughter Deonna Sky a plate too. I can hear them two upstairs playing with *Thomas The Train* figurines and watching another episode of Dora. I brush off the comment and help her fix plates. The kids get settled in and the rest of us fix a plate. Jamal eats upstairs like usual and Dee grabs a seat beside me on the couch. The two lil ones eat at the patio table, and get a reward for their clean plates. Dee gives each excited child a sugar free ice pop and refill's their Sippy cups with juice. At dinner they have to drink milk or water, but if they're good they'll get juice. It makes me so proud to see how good of a mom Dee is to her babies. I want to be like that with the one in my stomach. It's a vow I've always had before I got pregnant with Jayceon's baby. The hours pass. There are no missed calls or texts from Jayceon and Dee is asleep upstairs, so it's just me downstairs. I'm winding down from today, all of the excitement of baby classes and new houses, I need to go to bed because tomorrow will be busy. Dee is taking me to the parenting class if Jay forgets. I hope he doesn't, and it's only one day away from the funeral. I say my prayers for a brighter tomorrow and pass out.

Surprisingly Jayceon is out front and comes up to the door, he's here to take me over to the community rec center for Miss Maddison's parenting class. We go over and as I get out the car he yells at my back "Shawtie, I've gotta meeting with the weed man, so I'm finna swoop through. A'ight?!" I just shake my head in aggravation and walk up the stairs alone, once again, and hope that my new friend is here. We all file down the fold-out tables selection of free breakfast food and I grab a water and granola bar. I see Raquel in her same spot as last week. The seat on her left is taken and the one on the right has papers on the chair. She's probably saving it for her baby's dad. At least he came inside, unlike mines. Passing by her, she calls for me.

"Ay, Uhm, Chantell…here!" Moving the papers she smiles and tells me that she was saving me a seat. "Where's baby's dad?" She keeps looking at the door like she wants to rate him on a scale of one to ten when I inform her "he's busy this morning…so I'm here by myself. But, thanks for saving me a chair!" We chat about how the class seems fuller than the time before and Miss Maddison starts class. An hour passes and Jayceon calls me, so I step out in the gym's hallway.

"Yeah Jayceon, what's good?" My back is lined up against the cool white wall when he tells me "Shawtie, call Dee, cuz I can't pick you up. Niggas wanna think it's a game wif these bricks…I've gotta stay at the East Side trap mama but I will stop by and see you over at Dee's once I'm done!" I just brush him off and before we get off he asks me "Are you mad at me Shawtie? Cuz you know Daddy loves you, I'm just real sorry about this bullshit…" I tell him I love him and I'll see him later. I hang up and call Dee, but she ain't picking up. The class is over almost as soon as I sit down and I ask Raquel for a ride home.

"I know this is awkward because we just met, but could you give me a ride? Baby's dad is busy with shit and my other ride ain't picking up…" She just smiles and says "Yeah, I can give you a ride, where you need to go?" We talk the whole way out and get in her '93 Pontiac Grand Pre. It's a maroon piece of shit, but I can't talk too much shit because she's miss independent, yeah, Raquel's got her own.

"Is you hungry girl? Cuz if you is I got a little cash on me we can hit up a drive thru window…" She smiles and welcomes my warm invite, we head over to a little diner called not too far from Dee's. The wait-ress sits us down and Raquel and I act like we've known each other for years. It's crazy what type of bond we've already got. We order drinks and she starts to tell a little bit about herself-- more than Miss Maddison's class requires.

"I lost my first baby's dad to cocaine, he's addicted and is probably stealing somebody's microwave for that shit. The new baby's dad isn't a drug addict but addicted to the paper chasing, he's not a huge hustler but he keeps himself afloat without a nine to five job and shit..." I tell her about Jayceon and she seems impressed. "What, you're with that nigga Jayceon, Jayceon Michaels?! That dude really has street cred in these streets, damn. I'm dealin' with ah diva!" I smile and love when Jay's street rep makes me look like the hustler's wife that I am. I tell her about my mom who OD'd and how I lived with my Aunt. She tells me how she moved around from foster home to foster home, nobody wanted her and when her first baby's dad came along and paid her attention, she fell in-love instantly. Our sandwiches come over. I take a bite out of the spear dill pickle. It feels like we've been friends since back in the day. We keep sharing facts of our life when she asks me "Are you happy right now, where you're at with Jay?" It's hard to answer that honestly. On the outside it feels like we're perfect, but all the hus-tling and pill money makes me seem hesitant, Jay is gone now more than ever and I'm wondering if he's been faithful. I know how these bitches can be promiscuous.

"Eh, yeah, I guess...he's away more than I like, I've been staying with my sister Dee for a few days now..."

She asks me Dee's last name and I tell her. "Does she date a dude named Jamal?" I nod my head yes, and the she squeals "Jamal is my cousin's best friend. They used to be close as fuck--practically grew up together and shit! Damn, I know Dee too. She probably won't remem-ber me but when my cousin got locked up Jamal kept talkin' about his new chick Dee. She just got pregnant back then too." I tell her about her two babies Ja'mari and Deonna Sky. What a small world. We fin-ished our meals and we go over to Dee's. I invite her inside once I get the okay from Dee, and she hangs out for a few. The two of them catch up and Jamal can't believe that she's in his living room after all those years. His dude, her cousin, has been holding the cellblock down for going on seven years now. Free their nigga Rocky! It gets late and Dee puts the babies to bed after dinner and bath time. Raquel heads out around nine to go pick up her kid from the babysitter. "A'ight mama we'll see you later!" She waves and takes off into the night, Dee looks happy as hell and so does Jamal.

"Damn, Shawtie I can't believe ya'll got that class together, that's what's up!" Dee and Jamal pass the blunt and I don't even take a hit. Jayceon still hasn't called back. Oh well, fuck that nigga.

Lil Trae's funeral was peaceful and horrible. It was a closed casket, but the mood felt too fucking tense. Jayceon and his main niggas are on deck with the heat if someone tries to steal another one of our players from the team. I was sad to lose my best friend and brother. It was a shame to see his mama clinging to the casket, but my little bro was in peace. He wasn't at war with other gangs, fiends and those pills. He was surrounded by God I'm sure. I wore an all-black matching pant suit, Dee had a cute but respectful dress and Jamal had a dress shirt and slacks, he wasn't a part of Jay's main clique so he didn't rock the same fresh air-brushed RIP shirt and dark denim jeans. Jayceon showed up with Killa Kam and we all met up outside to smoke a square. We all recall memories of Lil Trae, the good and some of them bad. My eyes are red from crying all morning. It's almost three o' clock, that's when we're having Lil Trae's burial. A cop escorts our cars in the usual fashion and I end up riding with Jayceon. It's a silent ride with just sounds of me crying and shaking. He touches me on my thigh to tell me it's alright and I shove his hand off. "Don't fucking touch me brah!"

If we weren't in a line for a funeral burial he would've swerved to the side of the road and started a confrontation. "What's yo' problem bitch?" He hisses.

"You are my Got-Damn problem...that's what it is..." He just shakes his head and mashes on the gas, telling me this is why he doesn't like me kicking it with Dee for days at a time. I let him know before we get out "It's not Dee or Jamal that has me pissed at chu; it's your actions nigga. You just think that you can pay me off to be a good wifey. What are you really doing on these late nights at the trap? Huh?!" I slam the door, Jayceon hates that shit and I go find Dee under the windy tent. We all crowd around as the pastor says his final words in front of Trae's casket. His mom is up front, me and Dee are a row behind her, she's crying so hard she's literally on her knees. The service ends and I grab a rose off the flower arrangement and walk over to Dee's car. Jamal is in the driver's seat with the car started and I can see Jayceon looking for me. He must have seen Dee in the passenger's seat because he's making his way through the wind and snow, and stepping over people's graves in a quick hurry. Dee keeps my window up but rolls her's down. "Yes, can we help you?"

Jayceon is fit to be muthafuckin' tied when he grits his teeth and says "Tell Chantell to get her ass out here and get in the car with me! I know she in here..." Dee just shakes her head and I scream from the backseat.

"No, Jayceon I'm going home with Dee and Jamal...notchu nigga, so get gone. You've got work in the streets anyways, so I'll have company with Dee."

Jayceon is trying to not make a scene when he threatens me one more time to get out before he opens the four door up and pull me out. "Nigga, fuck you. I'm out of chere'!" Jamal takes off. The confrontation gave enough time for everyone to get back in their warm cars and take off. I look back and see Jay standing in the snow walking to his car so pissed he could make the snow melt. I'll pay for this later, but right now, I'm not too concerned about it. I've got my real family and friends; that's all that me and the baby need.

A FEW MONTHS LATER

Raquel was out front of our new crib ready to pick me up for Miss Maddison's class at the usual time. "Chantell, why can't I take you for once?" Jayceon asked me as I threw some last minute shit in my purse.

"Because, baby, you're a business mayne. I'm finna go to this class and go to Dee's later. I'll be home by dinner. Plus I got my blackberry on me, so call me if you need me after class." I kiss him goodbye. He doesn't know it's all just an act. We'll get to that in a few. My girl swoops me up and we're off to class. This week we're using each other or our significant others as partners to practice breathing techniques and a walk through of what the "usual" labor process is like.

"Ay mama what's up? How you doin' this morning?!" Raquel smiles and pulls out the driveway saying "I'm straight! Damn, Jay really did move ya'll out tha hood huh!? Must be nice to not hear gun shots, sirens and seeing the zombie fiends just walkin' around all day and night."

I tell her that I kind of miss it. "It's boring here boo, ain't shit to do 'round here unless yo' play some kind of sport or are in ah fancy wine club. Ay, after we finish class you wanna go to Dee's again?"

Raquel agrees and says "Yup, then we can perfect our plan and get shit set up. I can't believe you even thinkin' bout leaving Jayceon. What if he tries to find you, like go on ah man hunt or some crazy shit?!"

I reassure her "That nigga wouldn't know where to look first, the only family I got is here so he's not going to even have a clue which state I fled to. You know." Miss Maddison's class was easy today, I got to lay on Raquel half the time and she laid on me in-between my legs, so we could all practice labor breathing. Raquel kept clowning on Miss Maddison whispering, "Bitch when yo' ass in labor yo' ain't goin' be breathing like that! Tuhh, you goin' be screamin' get me a goddamn epidural and pray to God that yo' alive after this!" We kept laughing and Miss Maddison gave us dirty looks. She was sick of our trifling asses in here clowning. We didn't care. Raquel and I left early. We had more shit on our minds than labor pain as we jumped on the freeway to go see Dee.

"Ay mama what's good? What's good Roc? C'mon in…I got lunch made!" Deonna ran past us and Dee reminds her there's no running in the house. The two sisters pile up beside each other on the couch and argue over watching Dora or SpongeBob.

"Mmhmm…smells good as hell in here Chef Dee!"

"Thanks boo, ya'll already know I gotchu some good ass food!" We all stepped in closer and could smell tacos and we can see all of the needed condiments on the counter. Shredded lettuce, tomatoes, cheddar cheese, and ranch dressing wait for our arrival.

Raquel asks "Did the babies, yo', and Jamal eat yet?"

"Yeah Roc, we all did. Go on and getchu as much as you want!" We start to fill our steaming tortillas with veggies and taco seasoned meat when Dee asks "Are ya'll really feelin' to leave and go hide out? Where the hell is Jayceon at by the way…?" Roc fills her in about Jayceon taking a trip over to a conference meeting with his connect in Indianapolis.

I chime in "Yeah, he leaves about two weeks from now. That will give us time to plan today and talk to your connect in Georgia…"

Dee just nods and says "when does he get back from his connects spot?"

"My due date is June 18th. So he should be back four days after I have my lil mayne!" I would have been excited to have a boy, so I could name him after my husband, but with this plan set, I won't have a husband anymore, no more fiancé and no more ride-or-die Chantell. The plan is to meet up with Dee's connect in Georgia, Andre, who moved his small family and wife into a town close to Atlanta called Ringgold. Roc and I are packing up as much shit as we can in her tiny Pontiac and taking our babies. We're moving to a better place to raise our kids and just get a fresh start with life. I still have mixed emotions about it honestly, but with the baby being so close to being born, it's helped me realize what my priorities as a mother should be. Dee, Roc, and I have had so many late night talks about all of the what-if's, if we decide to stay. I've weighed my options and I've tried not to factor my heart into the decision when it comes to Jayceon. Throughout our teenage years Jayceon and I have always had a love-hate relationship and that's okay if it's just us, but when you bring kids into this world, they don't need to grow up seeing their daddy hitting their mom. I don't want my kids to struggle and fight like Dee and I did with my mom and her mom. There is more to life than that. At least Roc and I hope so. I plan to go to school and make something of myself. Raquel talks about that same shit too. She want's to be a vet or a pre-school teacher. I haven't decided what I want to be, who I want to blossom into and whole-heartedly, if I really want to leave Chi-town. It's all I've ever known in life and anything else would be a huge change. Am I ready for that? Will I get over Jayceon or will he always stay in the back of my mind late at night? What if our son looks and acts just like him? Dear God, I'd have a handful!

"Bitch, is you listening?" I shake away from my thoughts and tune back in.

"No…I was too busy-"

Dee cuts me off and says "Too busy thinkin' bout Jayceon and shit!" The girls laugh and the kids in the other room mimic us.

"Nah, but fo' real what was we talkin' bout cha'll?!"

Raquel filled me back into reality. "Chantell you have to be committed to leaving. We can't get to Ringgold and then you get Horney or heartsick and just up and leave, okay?!" I nod my head. Damn it hurts and that food didn't help. "Yeah, I know Roc."

"No, it's more than "you know." You have to promise me Chantell, cuz I'ma tell yo' ass what, this shit is ah lifestyle, ah high off of hustlin' and illegal money. This shit is a cycle…" As soon as she said the word cycle it brought me back to that damn nosey nurse. Roc is starting to sound like her now. She needs to just shut up and hand me a business card. Maybe I would call that number now.

Dee adds her two cents saying "Yeah, Chantell, if ya'll going to bounce out…yo' best not come back unless yo' wanna end up where Lil Trae's at! Yo' know out of all of us how Jayceon don't play dat shit and once you come up missing he's going to do more than flip. Especially since you've got his one and only son. Shit, it's ah rap! All games aside Chantell are yo' really going to promise and commit to this shit or do you just want to stay and live life in hell with ah hustler?"

I stick up for Jayceon saying "Life with him isn't hell."

Roc throws a fist on the patio table and yells "then why the fuck are you leaving? You're not sick of the slaps and hair pulling? Yo' don't despise his ass when he screams in your face and fucking makes *you* say sorry when *you* didn't do shit in the first place? You're *okay* with him deciding when it's okay for him to be home and choosing who you're allowed to hang out with?" I take in all of her words and it helps me see a little better. Yeah, I have been living in hell. Instead of defending him I just start to cry. Tears slide down my caramel face and Dee pats my back. "See, the shopping sprees and Coach bags don't fill that void you're missing Chantell, only love from a *real* nigga will cure it, and of course some time. Time heals all things, 'member that's what Aunt Glenda used to say..." I have finally hit rock bottom, I see that a new house can't fix old issues. A new Coach purse can't replace the fact that he disrespects me in several different ways throughout the day. A baby boy won't cure his hustlin' ways.

Chapter Sixteen

We took Dee to class because she wanted to get out of the house. It's one of our few classes left before twenty-five people become parents real soon. Miss Maddison's cherry ass self is doing her usual speech about bottles, burping, and breast feeding when I get this sharp pain. My ribs have been bothering me for months, so I try and grit my teeth and get through it. My oversized belly hides my kitty but for some reason I feel wet, like I just pissed on myself. I excuse myself and go to the bathroom. I'm mad as hell that I did this. I've already pee'd my pants probably ten times plus throughout this whole pregnancy ordeal. Pulling down my maternity jeans I see fluid everywhere and I'm worried because it looks like water but smells like blood. "Fuck!" I race out of the restroom and back around the corner when I go scream for Dee. "Dee. Roc. Help me!" They both jump up and race from their metal fold out chairs. The whole class tries to get a glance of where I'm at from the hallway. They start to wonder out loud if I fell or if I collapsed. One ghetto-ass white bitch named Tami asked if this was the end of class! I should go punch that bitch in her face, but I've got to take care of me and mines so she's lucky. Dee and Roc zoom in and get me to my feet. This is one time I'm glad Miss Maddison's here.

"Chantell are you okay? Did you fall?!" Miss Maddison's calm ass asks me.

"Nah, I didn't fall. There's just this fluid errywhere and it looks like water but smells like blood"

She congratulates me and says "Chantell you're water broke honey!" A crowd starts to form and contractions start. Dee's big ass damn near carries me to the car and we're on our way to the hospital. My baby boy is on the way. I'm an emotional wreck. How bad does this shit really hurt?! Roc is in the back cheering me on, rambling on how she's excited that my baby's on the way and all I can think of is breathing. Not Jayceon. Not Dee weaving through traffic. Not on our plan to leave, a plan that I'm secretly debating on. I'm just focused on making it alive, safe, and hopefully pain free to this damn hospital! I'm in the wheel chair and all I can yell is I want some pain meds, give me some fucking pain meds! When this blonde haired nurse with a friendly smile pushes me to the maternity floor and keeps asking for basic info. They get me settled into a room. They give me a tranquilizer to help calm my ass down and the nausea, which isn't enough, and a cup of ice water. Dee and Roc are beside my bed. They shopped around the gift shop and bought three balloons, a huge vase of flowers, and each got a candy bar. "Where's mines at?" I stare at both of them chomping away.

"We ain't getchu one mama...you're supposed to eat those ice chips." Dee busts out laughing. She knows that I hate to eat ice because my teeth are too sensitive for that shit. I told Roc about the ice chips and called a nurse with my buzzer. The intercom asks me what I need and I tell her. "Ay, I need some type of food, I'm starvin' up in dis bitch, ya feel me!?" The girls laugh and so do I but I add at the end that I'm serious, I'm not playin'. A new nurse introduces herself and tells me that I can't eat right now. They'll get me food in a few and I just need to focus on sitting here and staying calm. I'm busy cussing under my breath, fuck it, and decide to shoo her off. Roc asks if I'm going to let Jayceon know that I'm in here. I shrug my shoulders. I could call him and tell him, or I could ignore him, but that's too hateful. We're bringing a boy into this world and I didn't make this baby all by myself, I do need to call him.

"Jayceon Michaels where you at babe?" He already sounds irritated.

"At the East Side crib where you at?" I hear some bitch in the background, did she just kiss him on his neck? Oh hell nah!

"In the mother fuckin' hospital and yo' best stop tellin that ho to stop kissin' on yo' daymn neck! Nigga think I'm playin'!" He starts to deny it and asks me why I'm in the hospital. I fire back "Why the fuck do yo' think I'm here? I'm having your son and you've got the nerve to be laid up with some bitch, really Jayceon?! I swear ta God-" He hangs up.

Dee and Roc acted like they didn't see me flip my shit and try to change the topic. I just start screaming that "I hate him" when Dee slides over beside me and just hugs me. Tight and warm while she shushes me.

Whispering loud enough for Roc to probably hear she tells me "baby, you've got more to worry about than that dude cheating on you. You're getting ready to have a son who needs a mommy and I know damn well you're going to be a good one! Stay strong Shawtie. You can do this, lil mama and fuck the rest!" She kisses me on the top of my head and confirms what I've always known. "We're always here for you. I promise you that Chantell!"

Jayceon Trae'von Michaels was born later into the next day on June 17th. I struggled with the labor pains in the beginning, I think I was just flipping out. Once I got in the rhythm and stayed focused… there he was. My baby boy was born with a good amount of black hair covering the top of his head. My soft brown eyes couldn't move off of my new bundle of joy, the one whose about to change *my* life for the better. His nose looked like Jay's and his lips were cute like mine. Jayceon wasn't here to cut the cord so I let Dee do the honors. Hell, I know that Dee will always be with me, unlike that trifflin' nigga Jay. I spell out my baby's name for the birth certificate and I know that white nurse had to shake her head and make some racist remark about how black people name their kids. This baby's name had meaning just like the baby himself. Jayceon came up to the hospital and couldn't believe that I already had him.

"You already had the baby?"

Roc tells him where the baby's at "Yup. They cleanin' him up and errything, ya'll make cute babies!" She laughs but she's the only one laughing. Jay keeps questioning me.

"Who cut the cord?"

"Who do you think? It sure as hell wasn't yo' ass!"

"Okay smart-ass, see there yo go with that dumb shit! Who the hell cut it, was is Dee or this chick?" Jayceon just points to Roc not even looking her way. He's never met her. He carries on saying "Why didn't you tell me that you were this close to havin' him? It is a boy right? Have you given them the name yet?"

"I'm not on no dumb shit, nigga yo' shouldn't of been laid up in the trap with some ho on yo' neck, and, yes Dee cut the cord. I called and toldchu Jay dat I was having him…and yes it's a baby boy. I named him."

Before I can reveal the name he gets mad as fuck. Dee finally tells him to calm his ass down and listen.

"If yo' ass woulda gave me a chance to talk and finish…I named the baby Jayceon Trae'von Michaels. Whatchu think Daddy?"

He's speechless when he walks over to my bed and we French kiss. Dee talks shit about PDA.

"Mayne, shut the fuck up Dee! Ya old ass always got some bullshit to say. C'mon now!" Jayceon glares over his shoulder at her sitting on the plastic coated rocking chair.

Dee starts to go in on him but we hear a nurse walk in and our baby is crying. She asks if Jay is the Daddy and we both say yes. "Here is your new bundle of joy!" The look on Jayceon's face says it all. He seems like a different man. Roc and Dee make their way to the hallway and give us a family moment. It's times like this that make me not want to leave, Jay's already got lil mayne asleep on his chest. Tears sweep across his face. He can't believe that we finally have our baby here who's healthy and safe. We kept talking about how it all went down in the delivery room when Jay's phone chirps. He gives me a sorry face and answers. "It's Jay, what up?" He doesn't say another word and just walks to the hallway. Dee and Roc pile back in. The baby is now in my arms and as quick as the feeling of love came, abandonment came even faster.

"Where did Jay go?" Roc asks and all I can do is shake my head. I try to play my tears off as happiness for the baby, but I knew they were for Jayceon. I was going to miss him, more than I really had thought. Having a baby made it so much harder, *damn it.*

I wake up and freak out. Its weird waking up in a hospital. Dee is on the pullout couch texting on her phone and Raquel isn't in the room. "Ay sleepy head yo' ass finally wake up?" I sit up a little bit and ask where the baby's at. "Oh, they let him sleep with the other ones tonight. They said you were too exhausted to take him home tonight so we goin' post up in here tonight mama. Do you care if I'm up here withchu?"

I told Dee I didn't care but I was curious where Jayceon was at. She could see that look of worry when she informs me "Jay had to go re-up the 'dro and pills at the traps" she whispers. I asked why. When in the hell did we start selling shit that quick?

Dee asks me if I feel okay and if I'm hungry. I tell her I'm okay and I'm too pissed and disappointed to eat. Fuck that dude Jay. I swear if I wasn't tangled up in these IV's and in a hospital gown I would probably punch him straight in his shit. Dee takes this opportunity to show me, first hand, what the next eighteen years could be like. Starting with right now.

"Shawtie, I don't have to get on you or scream at chu to show you where your relationship with Jayceon is at. But, I do know that if you decide to leave, yeah it seems hard, but I promise it will be easier with time."

"Dee it's not like that, I know I need to leave but how can you leave someone that you've already fallen in love with, got proposed to, had a baby together and deep down depend on him for everything? I don't have a GED or no fucking college degree Dee…"

"That's why yo' and Raquel go to my spot in Georgia. Andre goin' make sure ya'll get on your feet and help you figure everything out. If you want to do GED classes he can set it up, if you're serious about a job he can pull some strings. I've known Andre my whole life, he's trustworthy."

"But Dee what if-"

She cuts me off saying "But what? Hell wouldn't you rather have an adventure, escape from this hustlin' life forever or even just awhile? Be thankful that you've got the chance because I never got that. Do you see how me and Jamal are? Do you notice we go our separate ways most of the day?! Do you want that to be Jay and you on a good day? Aren't you sick of all the physical fights and screaming? Don't you think the baby would like silence over screams? It's time to grow up Chantell Saunders." Before I can even open my mouth to defend my relationship, Dee hushes me. "I don't wanna hear your excuses. I don't wanna hear the lies and I'm not hearing the bullshit. Sit here and think about what you want in life, what's best for you and yours and I'll see you in a few hours. Get some sleep ma."

Not even hugging me she steps past my bed and I feel like Deonna who got disciplined. I just sat there and kept thinking. Hell, I even made a pro and con list. My list looked like this:

Pro's: Keep our family together <3, Stacks on deck, Iced out, weed and fresh gear, Jayceon's love, a new house and profitable trap houses.

Con's: Screaming and cussing, abusive, holding grudges, fighting in front of the baby or family/friends, being dependent, not having my own job or vehicle. Not having a GED or college classes. Crying. Tired of the hos calling my phone, fighting them and proving that I am the real Mrs. Michaels.

I wrote my name out in fancy writing. Chantell Michaels. I scribbled hearts around it and made it look cute but after I kept reading the Con's section and hearing Dee's voice in my head I crossed out the hearts. That nurse from the ER came into my mind when I scratched out "Michaels" and her words kept replaying in my head. I need to end this cycle. They're right, I need to do it for me and baby Jayceon. I need to do it for Lil Trae. I need to do it to start over and have a new life. I don't want to end up like Dee and Jamal on a good day. There's no fucking way. I find my phone and text Dee.

"Mama, I been up thinkin' and yo' ass is right! Tell Raquel I'm ready <3".

Chapter Seventeen

*I*t feels good to be out of the hospital especially with baby Jayceon Trae'von wrapped in my arms. Dee helps me into the car and Raquel was in the back. They cooed and made over my little angel and I let Raquel hold him while I blaze an L that Dee snuck over to me. Don't judge me ya'll when I'm blazing with my son is in the back seat, I've got some stress and shit on my mind and I'm about to make life changing choices, so if I need to hit some 'dro to help me stay calm and think clearly, then that's what it is! Dee takes us over to this little pizza joint for lunch and it seemed weird holding a baby and carrying a purse. People say that motherhood will become natural and don't get me wrong it does, but I guess it goes back to me depending on Jayceon. Someone to be there and help me along the way with the baby. I'm not used to being by myself, but I guess I need to get prepared real fucking quick. Inside Coalfire off of W. Grand Avenue, we start to discuss our plan. It's safer being over by the West Side because Jay is either on the East Side or South Side. He hardly comes over to the West Side.

We all ordered some type of Pepsi product and Dee leads the conversation. "I called Andre last night and he says he's ready for ya'll to stay if you're still dedicated..."

Raquel chimes in "Wait. Wait...hold the hell up, where does this nigga Andre stay at? And we ain't feelin to be on no pimp and trick shit!" She moves her hand between me and her showing Dee that we ain't down for that type shit!

Rolling her eyes she says "Ya'll really think I'm goin' do you like dat? C'mon now! Nah, this dude Andre is cool as hell. We grew up together and now he is happily married with three kids. They live in a suburbanite area in Ringgold, Georgia. It's right before ATL. If anyone needs to know you guys are his cousins moving down here to stay with family." Damn, Dee really has been thinking about this shit. Nice cover up. "Now ya'll got any other questions before I finish?" We let Dee continue while she lays out how the plan will work. "Jayceon will be at the East Side trap tomorrow, correct?" I agree. "So, tonight is when you pack up all of the baby's new stuff, formula, bottles and then worry about your stuff. He won't be home. He'll be too busy in the streets and that will give you ah head start. While he's over there we can get the ball rolling. This is when you and Roc pack all the bags up in her whip the next morning. When you're packed up, then stop by my house and get this envelope. It has contact information like my number, Jamal's and directions. There's a few hundred in it as well. It's the most that we could spare in the recent months." I asked how many miles it would take to move from my comfort zone into new territory. Dee chimes in "It will be around six hundred and forty miles, not counting the pit-stops or gas fill-ups. It's going to be roughly nine and a half hour trip, after a few hours you'll get to a town in Indianapolis called Lebanon. It's a simple drive, ya'll just going to get on highway 65 South."

Roc adds "Okay, that sounds easy...but why don't we up the stakes." We all look at her like this bitch thinks it's a game, I don't want to die tomorrow... "What?!" we squeal. Roc looks like a gold-diggin' bitch when she spits "Rob dat nigga! He got stacks on deck and Chantell know that...take some of that cake for all them fights, smacks and all the hell he done put you thru!" Our appetizers come and lil mayne starts crying so I pick him up out of his brand new car seat and rock him. "Shhh...it's all good baby boy...mama goin' getchu far away." It even felt weird just saying those words let alone living them. Mozzarella sticks and Antipasti salad get passed around. "How much do you really think Jayceon has on him Chantell?" I chew some antipasti and swallow. "Well, I mean, if we don't touch the drugs he's probably got around two hundred thousand in cash. If we fucked with the drugs we'd probably have damn near well close to a million..." I drench more ranch on my food as I still rock the baby and bounce him a little. The girls debate on taking the drugs too or just the cash when a deep dish pizza comes our way. Peperoni and cheese, my favorite, and we all dig in. Still unsure of a solid plan we're all going through with it, tonight I have to pack up the outfits, bottles and formula for Jayceon Trae'von and get my shit together...what if Jay comes home early? We put the leftovers in a box and Dee drops Raquel off at her place then takes me home by ourselves.

"Chantell, are you sure that you're ready for this type of change?" Baby Jayceon cries and I just say yes to prevent hearing her mouth. Am I really ready right at this moment? No. I still have the flicker of hope that we can work it out, the violence will stop and our cycle will change. But, that's not reality. If it was going to change it would have years ago and that's just a fact that I have to dwell on down life's road. It's time to put my feelings aside and do what's right for my baby boy and myself. I know that Lil Trae would be proud that lil sis is leaving the cycle and creating a better life.

"How are you sure that he won't be home? Cuz it'd be my damn luck that he'd show up wanting to make-love or fuck and be the mayne of the house for the night..." Dee told me she took care of that, she didn't say how, but she just guaranteed that he would be busy. "You didn't kill him did you?"

"Hell nah, we don't want him dead we just want him farthest away from you and my godchild as possible. Trust me. He'll be busy tonight and he won't even think about you or the baby. He's doing okay, just a little preoccupied." I get out of her whip and we're back in the suburbanite project with the welcome mat that reads "The Michael's".

Chapter Eighteen

I've been packing up baby Jay's stuff and folded all his clothes up, not neat, but just stuffing them into different purses and a few duffel bags. My closet looks bare like the first day that we moved in. I remember how excited I was to have a walk-in closet. Jayceon was promising me the world and all the safety that I could imagine. I can still here him saying "We made it out the hood mama. Toldcha ass I'd getchu here, didn't I?" We made love the first night we moved in and the next few days after that, but by the time a month had hit he was back on his hustle full time. It's like I was already a single mother and I hadn't even had baby Jay yet. The dresser looks abandoned and I feel like I'm abandoning everything that I've ever dreamed of. All I wanted was to be with Jayceon Michaels, and I did that. Wifey, I'm there and baby's mom, we made that happen, but I never imagined that I would be leaving. Turning the T.V. on for noise, I hate being alone in this big ass house. I just keep packing and pray that our plan goes through okay and I just keep telling myself that it's for a better life. Why did it take me so long to see through the "love" what Jayceon really was? All he is, is ah hustler, just like the other men in and out of my life growing up. I guess that's all I've ever known. Baby Jay is sleeping but I hear him start to cry and rush over to the bed; he must be hungry. "Hi mama's boy! Shh, stop cryin' for mama, yo' hungry? Huh? Mama goin' have to go make you a bottle, c'mon lil mayne." I take him downstairs, rocking him on my chest and patting his diaper and fix him a bottle. I feel exhausted and we aren't even on the run yet. I feed baby Jay his bottle and he settles down, almost drifting back off into dream world, and I wish I could curl up too and fall asleep, wishing this could all be just a dream. It's raining, pouring hard and I've got just about everything packed and hidden if Jay would come home. I've been thinking of excuses in case he does swoop through, just to save my ass. I need some reassurance so I give Dee a call.

"Dee...whatchu up to?" I'm still stuffing clothes and some jewelry into a Louie V bag.

"Nothin' really, I just put the kids to bed and Jamal left, I'm bout to call Andre and tell him we're down to head out. When do you want to get on the road with Raquel?"

"Uh, well probably early because I have no clue when Jayceon would show up...I know that he don't get up usually before noon or one...does that help any?"

"Okay, yeah that helps. Roc said that ya'll should leave tonight, hit the road and keep going. There wouldn't be any traffic out really and you'd get ah good head start before he even wakes up, ya feel me?"

"Oh...yeah..." I didn't know what to really say.

"C'mon I'm finna call Roc and we goin' swing through and put all the bags in her whip, then we can decide mama!" I know that I should be that excited but there's still a huge piece of me wanting to just scream that I'm staying and that's life. But, I have more than just me to think about now, and I need that to be my main priority.

"A'ight den, I'm finna have baby Jay T. ready and we'll be waiting, hurry yo' asses up though! No stops on the way for food or nothin' cuz I'm nervous than ah muthafucker!"

Dee laughs and we get off the phone after she says she's proud of me and she'll see me in a few. I start to move all my gear in hiding and put it by the front door. Roc pulls into the driveway and they both help me load up all the stuff in the trunk. I keep taking deep breathes to help calm me down, It's really happening, I'm leaving Jayceon Michaels. I'm leaving the love of my life, fiancé, baby's dad and the one who's been my everything for the last five years.

Chapter Nineteen

Chantell's at the crib, I'm stepping out the whip over at the trap. "What's good Fam?" I gave some dap to Killa Kam.

"Not shit, just another day in the trap, we stay sellin' tha werk nigga! You know" I'm acting fake as fuck to Kam, ever since he fucked my main bitch I know that I can't trust that dude but due to the drug ring we've got, I let him keep his position in the trap for now. He's still on my suspect list for whoever killed my brother Lil Trae. If I find out he did it, well no matter who did it, they or he is goin' get that heat and look like Swiss cheese! We went over numbers at the East Side and talked about the South Side trap too, I needed to keep these numbers up and had to figure out how to keep these fiends coming back. Right now, I'm focused on finding out what happened when me and Shawtie was out of state, why did our crib get hit on?

"Ay, brah, yo' know anything about the trap headquarters above Rick's getting hit?" Kam lights up a pearled blunt and we start rotation. "Nah, nigga, I didn't see anything about it. I just heard from that crack head Reeci…she told me she went over there to get her usual shit and she seen the door kicked in. She gave me some sob story that she hoped Chantell was okay, cuz she knows that yo' Shawtie stay there by herself sometimes…Reeci investigated shit and told me that she saw Lil Trae just laid out on the floor, blasted." As soon as Kam said "blasted" it took me back to being at Trae's funeral and seeing the closed casket, watching his mama flip out and seeing my baby's face full of tears from losing her brother. I've gotta find dese bastards who killed my nigga! We change the subject because I can feel my stress level rise, so we hop in the whip and pick some food up. I pay cash for our drive-thru visit at Mickey D's and we each get two sweet tea's. It'd be a while before we leave the trap because I've gotta find a replacement for Lil Trae's spot. No, there will never be a street soldier like Trae, but I need someone to watch over our old crib and someone that knows how to do the shit we do. I guess I'm doing interviews today, my blackberry been blowin' up all damn day to get his spot. We've got a few candidates and I've already got in my head who I'm going to choose, but I ask Killa Kam like I'm unsure.

"Who we goin' find to fill in Trae's spot over at Rick's?" Between bites of his McDouble he tells me "Dat nigga Jon…he's got the streets on lock for being on his side of town fo 'real!"

"Mayne that nigga ain't got shit on lock, he lets his main bitch run shit! He's ah bitch-ass nigga fo' dat, cuz I know ain't no bitch goin' run me!"

Kam starts teasing me about baby mom's Chantell runin' shit.

"She don't run shit, yo' see she listen to Daddy when I speak. She'll jump high too if I make her."

"Yeah right, you do everything she be sayin' brah! She wanted to have kid, bam. Baby mom's status. She wanted to move out the hood, now look at cha'll movin' in with all dem rich white folks! She needs shopping money, hair money, nails money, pantie money, she ain't even gotta ask yo' just give it to her like a got-damn ATM machine! Bitch gotchu played out fo' real cuz."

I deny his bullshit claims, but I knew that I'd give or do anything for Chantell to keep her, our love whirlwind relationship and plus she's the only bitch who can be trusted with the scales, weight, money and I'll know it'll be there when I get home. She ain't no addict and she don't really drink unless we pop bottles, so for that Shawtie is a queen in my eyes and I try to keep her flossin' like one too. After twenty minutes I drive us over to Ray-Ray's on the South Side to see how he's doing. Check on numbers, see what I need to re-up on and just check to see if there's been any more incidents since that crazy white bitch talked 'bout stayin' strapped.

"Ay what's good Ray-Ray?" Killa Kam gave him dap and so did I. We all light up our own cigarettes while Ray-Ray multi tasks and rolls a new blunt too. We talk about that white bitch from a few months ago and determine that she ain't bout that life. We talk about how none of us can believe Lil Trae ain't here to pop another pill or drink his Goose and Hawaiian Punch mix or yellin' at his side bitch about talkin' shit to one of us. Laughing at the good times, harping on the bad times, and vowing to find the crew or nigga that did this, time passes by. Hell it's been five hours and we all blazed out. I check on the pills, weed and blow and see that it needs a little replenished. I go to the 300 and grab some pills and a brick of coke. The weed is already inside, you know we had to make sure it was some fiyah before we sold it! Ray-Ray give us dap for coming through and let us know his choice for who should be moved up the ranks.

"Ya'll know that dude Jim? Yeah that dude keeps his hustle up hard and knows how to keep fiends in check! I'm not sayin' he can replace Lil Trae, but he'd be ah good start..."

"Who he ryde with now?"

"He's doing his own hustle by the West Side, sometimes he'll hit me up and try to get me on his team, ask how sales are doing and shit. I bullshit him though, but, he seems like ah good dude." Kam tells him we'll keep him in mind and we cruise over to Rick's, check on shit and then we'll be back to the East Side. I should stop by the new house and see how Shawtie's doing but we're busy so I'll give her ah call.

"Ay boo what's good? What's yo sexy ass doing?"

"Aww, not shit, just taking care of the baby, you know..." She kept the conversation short when she said "Damn it. Jayceon I'ma call you back, the baby keeps crying..."

"Nah, Shawtie, you want me to come thru and give you some of this late nite snack?" She knew I was talkin' bout fuckin' but tonight she wasn't on it.

"Jayceon I'm so daymn tired, all I wanna do is get this baby to sleep and I'm goin' pass out. Daddy, stay in the trap and hustle for us, shit, it's better than being here!"

"You don't like our new house? See there yo' ass go, always gotta complain about shit and never be happy with what the fuck I get... Chantell I swear-"

"Shut the fuck up, I'm tired of you always playin' that blame game. I'm happy with what you got us, remember nigga it's for us, not just me. And besides you never come home anyway so don't play like it's ah treat just to have you lay beside me! I've got my toy when you're on the run so I'm not begging for the dick, I'm past them days withchu!"

Damn, what the hell is her problem? "Whatever bitch, I'll be home when I fuckin' get home then! I don't need chu either, Jayceon Michaels never begs for pussy, especially from a main bitch, tuh! That's the shit you say to me and wonder why ah nigga go and creep, these side chicks feel privileged to be with me, unlike yo' hateful ass! Yo' best get wit it or get lost cuz I'm not hearin' that type of shit for the next eighteen years..."

Before I can really go in on her she screams "Yo' ain't gotta worry about me for the next eighteen years, I might just get tired of yo' shit and leave...you never know nigga..."

"Yeah right Shawtie, nice play, but I know that ass ain't goin' nowhere, whatcha goin' go live with Dee and her dumb ass dude? You can't handle one baby so what makes you can handle her bad ass kids?" I kept laughing and she hung up. When I see her I'ma have to fuck her up for talkin' like that, I had her on speaker phone so Kam heard everything. We hit the East Side trap around six a.m. and there's business rolling through. Kam takes his spot as manager and I peep a cute lil mama on the porch. I spit her game like I did with Chantell, she knows who the fuck I am before I say my name so she was down to head upstairs. We fucked twice and I bust all over her face each time. It felt good to fuck ah freak for the night, but, it wasn't how me and Chantell did. No bitch could compare to her, so I had to keep her ass, why ya'll think that I gave her ah ring and a commitment? The baby this time was to keep her happy and give her a reason to stay, even when I act up and do shit wrong to her. The miscarriage from before was on purpose. I knew she was creepin' with somebody, I just never imagined it would be Killa Kam. He's goin' get his soon, and she will too if she even thinks about leaving.

Chapter Twenty

Dee gave me the hugest hug that I could even imagine and even kissed my cheek. "Here's that envelope boo, once you get on the road check it out..." I told her I loved her and gave her the phone that Jayceon got me so long ago. "Here sis, if he comes looking for me he'll try to call. Don't answer it but keep it so I can get all my pictures and contacts out later, a'ight?" Raquel is already in the car and has her baby girl in her car seat beside baby Jay T. who's right beside her in his new car seat too. They would make a cute couple. The trunk is so weighed down that her Pontiac is saggin' like hustler's jeans do from all them bands in dey pockets. Dee waves at us while I pull out of the drive way, telling me to just hit highway 65 South, again, and then read the directions in a few hours. Fuck it, I know that I have to be making the right choice. If I stayed eighteen more years I might get locked up for killing that nigga, because there's so much hate there. Yeah, there was love obviously, but having Jay T. made me see that we we're stuck in the cycle and I needed the baby to give me the courage to leave. I have to let him have a better childhood than I had, like dealing with alcoholic family members, a mom on heroin, and having no one to turn to. Thank God he gave me Dee to see me through it all, but I can't depend on Jay T. finding someone to be his Dee; I've gotta make a change. Tears start to slide down my face as I kick it in on the highway. Roc fell asleep so we can take turns driving, but I pre-pared myself to drive the whole trip. Knowing that Jayceon's going to be more than pissed, I'm tryin' to avoid the pit-stops. Knowing him, he's probably letting some chicken head suck his dick right now. That's the grimy shit he does. He acts like Kam don't tell me, but nigga I've got ways to find shit out. *Why you think I don't want to really even lay beside chu? Yo' dirty like ah needle and I don't get down with that.* It's been a few hours of me talking to myself inside my head and we've already passed Chicago's state line. Now we're in Indianapolis. A green highway sign reads Indiana, only seven and a half hours until a new beginning

Chapter Twenty-One

I sped over to the new crib; Chantell was still on my mind from last night. Yeah, she talks a lot of shit, but after I let her know about herself, she won't be able to resist how I dick her down. I know she hears from the streets that I creep sometimes, but that shit ain't new to our relationship. Hell, what do you expect from one of Chi-Town's greatest? If she want some boring ass lame she better go find a dude with ah real nine to five who drives some type of Honda or Toyota. This nigga ain't settling down and since Lil Trae's death it makes me realize even more how short life is, so if I wanna let one or two, hell three bitches get a taste, it shouldn't matter. Chantell should stay happy that she has my first born and a new crib. She upgraded, unlike these other hos who stay downgraded.

The streets are like a ghost town at our new house. Pulling up I can see that her car is still in the driveway. I can't wait to see lil mayne, I'm finna take Shawtie and baby boy out to breakfast. We should go to IHOP or Cracker Barrel; lil mama likes those places. I pull up behind her whip and get out, still looking fresh since the last time I left. Unlocking the door, everything seems all good until I call out for her. "Chantell, Daddy's home!" I peep up the steps and I don't hear no movement. The living room is dead quiet; not even the T.V.'s on or music. I walk into the decked out appliance kitchen and the granite counter tops show no life. They're bare and the wooden floor has no baby toys on it. Hell, Chantell, was always good at keeping the crib clean. I skip up the steps, two at a time. I bet they're both asleep. I can wake Shawtie up with this tongue and…

"What tha fuck!" I didn't see Chantell in any of the rooms that I passed and the bedroom was empty. I looked around for her phone, nobody would've kidnapped her and my son, would they? I grab my heat out of the waist band and check each room. No one's in here. No note, no goodbye, no baby. The closet that she begged for is empty except my shit. Brand new J's stare back but the void of her missing clothes lets me see the paint on three of the walls. Now, I'm pissed and mixed up. I grab my phone and call hers. It went straight to voice mail. Slamming doors and cussing the whole way out, our next door neighbor sees me and starts to put up a wave while I hop in the 300. He frowns as I pull away with tires squealing and probably goes inside to tell his wife in his best fake hustler voice "That guy beside us was pissed. He's finna kill that bitch! I bet she cheated!" They'll probably laugh about it over tuna casserole or some shit. I pull up in front of Dee and Jamal's and I don't even tuck the heat. Fuck the police.

"Where in the hell is Chantell. She's not at the crib!" Jamal doesn't let me in. I push my way through that damn door and look for the other two. "Dee, Dee, getcha fat ass down here, right muthafuckin' now!"

She waddles her way down the hallway and piers at me from the top of the steps. "What nigga, daymn can't people sleep 'round here?" I tell her not to make me come up them steps when she decides to try and calm me down. "I ain't got no clue where she at! What I look like, her mama? Ask Jamal I been here all damn night in this boring ass house!" She rolls her eyes at Jamal but I'm not in the mood for games. The last time I talked to Chantell clicks in my head.

"She told me she was leavin' last time we talked so where'd my bitch go? Did she take my fucking son?" Dee didn't answer. She kept glaring while I pointed the chrome piece at her face. "Yo' best start talkin' bitch!" That was her cue to come downstairs. Jamal was on the porch and couldn't see me holdin' this heat at his ol' lady's face. Yanking her arm down the other two steps I push her ass to the couch.

She starts stuttering. "Ja-Ja-Jamal…" I backhand her to keep him from coming in. She tilts to the right side of the couch and starts cying.

"Bitch, save them tears for someone who cares. You talk to Chantell erry muthafuckin' day so I know if somethin' went down you already know where she'd go. Is she at another trap? Is she riding around the streets? But, why would she empty her whole closet and take my son to a shitty trap house? Yo' best be giving me answers you fat fucking slut!" Jamal stepped inside and saw the gun pointed at her and told me to calm down.

"Brah, calm down with all that killer shit! It ain't that serious. Chantell ain't here dude." I take the heat and aim it at his dome "Then where is lil mama, huh?" Jamal shakes like a bitch, I knew bitch was always in his blood, that's why he ain't never been accepted on my team. Holding his hands up like I'm arresting him he just keeps saying he don't know. I move the heat from one to the other and I finally get an answer. "She took baby Jay to go see family in North Carolina!" I kept thinking, hard, cuz Chantell don't have no family in any other state. This bitch is lyin' through her gapped teeth! That shit don't fly with me. I pistol whipped Jamal's weak ass and he damn near flew across the room. Dee gasps and tries to rush over to his side. Aww, how cute. "Nah bitch, sit that ass down. He be a'ight, lil nigga can handle ah hit!" Dee keeps looking out the corner of her eye, so I follow her sight and see a blanket on the recliner. Snatching it off the arm of the chair, this blanket looks familiar. It has my son's name stitched in bright blue across the side. "Jayceon Trae'von Michaels" in on the baby blue soft blanket. "I'm finna ask yo' dumb ass one mo' time where the hell my son is before I start emptying shells in muthafucker's. Think I'm playing? Huh? Don't make me shove this in yo' nasty fat mouth and make you suck it like it's ah dick…do you want that?" I grab the ponytail on top of her head and shove the gun in her face, making it slide across her lips like the base of my dick. The barrel gets to her lips and I hold it there, looking dead in her eyes, tears pour down her face and all she can say is "Georgia." I toss her whole face back and ask her "Georgia, that's where tha bitch fled to? Are yo' sure cuz if I send my goons out cha' and she don't come back… one ya'll bitches goin' die. Fuck, might as well be both cuz Jamal ain't even man enough to tell me to my face about shit. Punk bitch!" I kick him in his ribs and a good stomp to his face, the side that's still facing up from the other half resting in a small pool of blood. I storm out and call Killa Kam as soon as I'm in the 300.

"Did you know Chantell left? Don't fuckin' lie nigga!" He acts stunned but knowing their history I can't trust no one around me. They all jumpin' on that bullshit boat called "straight bitches". Over at the East Side I keep pacing and finally come up with a plan while the 'dro burns. I'll go find that bitch! Fuck sending my goons, this is *my* bitch and if I want her here, I'm finna go get her and my son. I call Ray-Ray and ask him "Ay brah is Shawtie from last night still dere?" He asks "which one? Redd, Gina or T'wana?" I tell him I want T'wana and he says she's sleepin' where I left her last night. "Tell her ass get ready, we finna go on ah road trip and pack her shit up." Before he can ask me where to or why he can't go I hang up. I'm parked out front of the South Side trap about an hour later and T'wana is sitting on the step with her legs crossed, a duffel bag that Ray-Ray must have had packed and smoking a Newport. I don't even leave the whip, I just roll the window down and holla at her.

"Ay Shawtie, c'mon get in if yo' ass leaving!" She smirks and throws her shit in the back, hops up front and we zoom off. Pulling a zip lock baggie of 'dro from her bra she asks if I got papers and I don't have any in the whip. We stop over at the Marathon and I send her in to buy some Zig-Zag and she grabs a few Red Bulls, Mountain Dew and a twelve pack of Budweiser. As we roll down highway 65 South, lil mama asks where we goin' and I tell her to pass the blunt. After a few hits I tell her.

"We've got to go find this bitch who took my son!" Hood rats, hos and tricks love a player who takes care of his kids or at least make it seem that way. It shows that I might take care of their ass if they listen and suck dick good enough. She gets higher than the sunshine and we keep the system banging while she gives me head as we whip through Nashville. She reminds me of Chantell in the beginning of our relationship. Shit, Chantell might have competition when I find her ass. She better hope I still got feelings cuz her ass could get easily replaced!

www.ingramcontent.com/pod-product-compliance
Lightning Source LLC
Chambersburg PA
CBHW020411150626
46554CB00013B/624